STATIC

STATIC

Tanya Lisle

Scrap Paper Entertainment

ISBN-13: 978-1-988911-13-7

Tanya Lisle
www.tanyalisle.com
Email: tanya@tanyalisle.com

Printed in U.S.A

CHAPTER ONE

WELL, THAT WAS uncalled for.

Harrison knew that he sometimes got a little immersed in what he was doing to the point where he didn't hear when Ally, his roommate, tried to get his attention. Usually she just took the book out from in front of him or cut off the Wi-Fi. Today, she decided the best tactic was smacking him in the back of the head hard enough that he slammed his face into the coffee table.

He groaned as he pushed himself back from the table, holding his now throbbing nose. He turned back, looking up at her with a mix of anger and confusion. *"What?"*

"Finally," she said, looking almost relieved. "I'll get you some water. Stay there. Don't get up."

"Ally, what the…"

Harrison's anger started to fade as he realized how sore his throat was from croaking out only those words. Slowly, he took stock of himself and his surroundings. His legs were completely numb underneath him and protested his movements. The coffee table in front of him was completely bare of anything that he thought he might have been working on. Or any food that he would have normally brought over to eat while he was studying. He was hungry and his throat was like sandpaper. He rubbed his face, feeling the barest hint of stubble that started to grow.

It could take a week before he started to feel stubble.

Confusion spread across his face as he looked around. At the door, there was Ally's suitcase and her coat thrown on top of it. Right, she wasn't supposed to be here right now. She was supposed to be back in Jersey with her family for the break. It couldn't be time for her to come back already, could it?

"How long have I been here?" he asked.

Ally handed him a cool glass before taking a seat next to him on the floor and watching him as he drank. She waited until the glass was back on the table, completely drained, before she spoke. "I think about three days," she told him. "It's Saturday. Do you remember where you were supposed to be?"

At first it felt like a trick question. Of course he knew where he was supposed to be. It had been the plan for weeks. He was...

"Oregon," she told him gently. "You went to Oregon for the break."

Harrison nodded. That sounded right. "Yeah, Oregon," he repeated, the hazy patchwork of something starting to come together in his head. "I was going to visit... I was visiting someone." He frowned, a crease knitting between his eyebrows as he tried to come up with who it was. It felt like he should know this. That this was an important person he was going for.

"Visiting your boyfriend," Ally told him. "Max Kani."

"Max," he repeated. A laugh came back first, and how much easier it was to bubble out these days. The red hair and splash of freckles which seemed to grow in number under the sun. Talking into the early morning on his living room couch. The stolen moments of intimacy carefully balanced with just how public Max was willing to make their relationship among his friends. The plans for Max to come out to Florida to visit him next, even though it was much easier for Harrison to go there.

He'd met Max more than a year ago while they'd been travelling the country with several more teens under very false pretenses. Harrison thought that they were trying to outrun the law after a shady organization had gone ahead and murdered their families in an attempt to get to them. It wasn't until well after Max had joined them, having been fed the same story, that they learned they had been lied to. They were actually being led to their deaths by a madman. They were lucky to get out at all, though it had taken a while for Max to recover.

Their relationship after they'd gotten home was slow, which suited him fine. They all needed time to adjust to just how much of their lives they had missed. Harrison had been gone a year by the time he returned home, and missed his last year of high school in the process. The company that sponsored their recovery, Harrish and Barrister, did what they could to get them up to date on their studies and ease them back into their regular lives, but it had come with the stipulation of a very long contract that they had signed without question.

They were not to talk about what had happened to anyone outside of the company. H&B wanted to know in as much detail what had happened while they were traveling the country, which entailed a lot of long meetings at the start of their tenure with the company. Harrison was fine with it, since it meant he would only need to go through it once and hopefully never again.

Aside from that confidentiality agreement, H&B also provided them with their choice of compensation for agreeing to continue to live by their rules. They would either cover schooling expenses or they would provide them a job in the organization. Harrison and Ally had both decided to take the education, though that had not been everyone's decision.

Harrison wasn't actually certain quite what else was in the contract. He knew that they had been called Metas, people with powers outside of the norm, and weren't supposed to reveal them to outside sources on penalty of their funding or positions in the company being revoked. Ally insisted that there was also a clause stating that if they had revealed themselves in an irreparable way they could also be subject to permanent imprisonment to maintain the confidentiality of the agreement. At least, that's what she said it said.

He also knew that they had all been assigned a Keeper to make sure that they didn't break any of the other rules. He lived with Ally partially because it made it easier for their Keeper, Emma, to keep an eye on them. So far, she had done little to stop them or interfere in their lives, so he assumed he was following their rules fine. Well, except for when she had to come by to remind Harrison that he had to go in for testing.

The testing had seemed innocuous at first. After all, Harrison had learned to teleport and it seemed like the sort of thing people would want to know more about. Per his contract, he was only to use his abilities when he was in view of only persons who also worked for H&B, and he was to go in once a week for them to see just how much he could do. Some weeks it was just a matter of checking out blood work, while others involved trying to figure out how much he could take with him how far across the country. It was exhausting, even though he decided long ago that he didn't want them to know just how much he could do and refrained from going all out on any of these tests.

His tests were nothing compared to what they made Max do. He had gone to spend the break with Max while he was in for another four day round of testing at their Oregon facility. Like every time he'd tried to be with Max during one of these, he watched as Max slowly grew more nervous and stressed while he was inside the facility. Max stopped sleeping by the second day, and kept looking over his shoulder for people that weren't there. He still remembered how Max jumped when anyone tried to touch him.

"Oh Max..."

"Do you know what happened?"

"I..."

Harrison frowned as his eyes went to the spot Ally was, finding her gone. She had moved to his other side at some point, now with a bag of chips in hand. She gave him the bag, but his hands had also gone numb. Massaging the feeling back into his fingers, he looked determined at the bag, his stomach aching for something to eat. "I remember he went in for testing with H&B," he said. "He... he wasn't doing so well. I don't know what they were testing him for. And then..." He could feel Ally's eyes on him, waiting for something specific. He tried to concentrate, trying to pull up the image of the very last moments he was there.

———◆———

HARRISON CAME TO see Max in the evening of the second day. They were half way through and already they had run out of things for Harrison to do, but Max was looking rough. Max hadn't been there for dinner, though Harrison knew he must be hungry after how much they had him locked away and doing whatever it was they were doing with him. He grabbed another plate for him and made his way to the small room with Max's name on it.

Max sat on the bed with his back against the wall, legs curled up with his chin resting on them. He didn't look up as Harrison came in, his eyes on the window but clearly not looking at it. His whole body wavered, his arms wrapped around his legs trembling like leaves caught in the wind.

He looked so fragile and Harrison didn't know what to do. H&B were supposed to be helping them, helping them figure out their powers and how to best utilize them going forward without creating a public outcry. He didn't know what purpose putting Max in this state could possibly serve and it hurt to see him like this.

Despite that, he was hit with a wall of fuzz settling in on his mind. Where his body might be weak, Max's mind was strong and echoing very loudly. It formed like a cloud around him when he was stressed, and while he was in here he seemed to be constantly stressed.

Luckily, Harrison had been with Max long enough that he could handle it, even when it was this strong. He set the plate down on the desk and went to sit down next to Max. "Hey," he said softly. "What did they do to you? Are you—"

Max jumped as Harrison let his shoulder drift a little too close. Harrison moved away, hand clenched into a fist to keep himself from reaching out to try and calm Max down as his trembling grew worse. They shouldn't be leaving him alone like this, but Harrison knew there would be no consoling him. Not until he was allowed out of here.

He thought about grabbing Max and running. It would be easy. They could—

"You can't break the contract," Max said absently. "They'll come after you for it. You'll never make it out."

"Only if they can catch me. They can't keep doing this to you."

"It's so loud. I don't know..."

Max had said that before, though Harrison wasn't sure what it meant. He knew Max could read minds to a degree, but Max insisted that wasn't where the loudness had come from. He said it was something else, that it seemed to be coming from inside of him and it was spilling out. Whatever it was, he knew Max didn't find it pleasant.

"He's coming," Max said, even his voice sounding hollow. "You need to go before he gets here."

"I'll be okay," Harrison said. He wanted to reach out, to hold him or touch him, to provide him some comfort, but Max already looked like he was about to run. "And so will you. We're going to be okay. Both of us. Who's coming?"

"He keeps finding me. He's getting closer. He's not happy."

"We could run," Harrison offered, inching closer. Max looked so small. So scared. He didn't know what was happening to him, didn't know how to help. He didn't know what H&B was doing to him. Didn't know what they were trying to prove or why they were putting him through this, but it couldn't be worth this. "You know I'm very good at that. I'll take you with me. We could take a nice vacation anywhere you want, maybe somewhere nice and sunny. Swimming in the ocean every day, far away from—"

Suddenly, Max grabbed his hand and looked directly at him, his eyes wide and desperate. "Just forget about me," Max told him. "Get out of here, go back and forget you ever knew me. Don't come back. Go have a good life, find someone who'll make you happy, and just stay away. Please, just... He doesn't want to see you again. Go and never come back."

HIS FACE FELL as the final moments came back. "He doesn't want to see me anymore."

"Yeah, that's not actually true."

"But he—"

"He called me when he got out," Ally said, speaking over him and cutting him off, keeping her eyes locked on his. "He was really worried."

"But did he *say* he wanted to see me?"

"Did he actually say he *didn't* want to see you again, or did he tell you to forget about him?" Ally asked. There was a familiar disdain in her voice as she said it. This was a conversation they had had before, and it was starting to feel repetitive, even to him. He knew this had happened before, knew he had felt this way about things before, and knew that Ally was growing tired of having this conversation every time Max sent him away during testing. "You need to actually call him, Harrison. Talk to him. It's not like this hasn't happened before. Where's your pho..."

Ally's phone rang and she pulled it out of her pocket, frowning as soon as she looked at the screen. "He always tells you to just forget about him, Harrison," she told him, getting to her feet as her eyes stayed on her screen. "And then you end up back here, forgetting that he exists until someone brings you back around. Every single time. No different this time. Hang on."

Harrison didn't know what to think. His hands had enough feeling in them, so he grabbed a handful of chips to satiate his hunger for at least a moment before reaching into his pocket for his phone. His ears were on Ally as she picked up her phone, his eyes on the screen in front of him telling him that he had only a sliver of battery left.

"What happened?" Ally asked. It must be Jaime. "What do you mean he's *missing*?"

Harrison felt Ally's eyes flicker to him before she turned away. She went quickly into the kitchen, her voice lowering enough that Harrison couldn't hear what she was saying anymore. He watched her pace back and forth before coming to a halt, her fingers rapping on the counter.

Something was wrong, he knew it. Harrison got to his feet, his legs still numb, and appeared directly behind her. He reached for the counter before his legs decided to collapse under him and leaned in close enough to hear Jamie's voice on the other end.

"... but Adam's in the hospital and it looks like they can't get in touch with Mary or Jack either."

Harrison froze behind her. Adam was supposed to watch over Max as well as Mary, Jack, and Ted in the same way that Emma watched Ally and Harrison. He shouldn't be in the hospital. He'd seen Adam and had determined that he, Emma, and Gavin were all damn near invincible.

"What about Ted?" Ally demanded, voice hushed.

"He doesn't know what's going on."

"But he's not missing too?"

"No, he's accounted for. So they aren't there?"

"I haven't talked to Jack since... since before. Or Mary."

Jamie went quiet for a long moment. "Okay. Call you back when I know more. Bye."

"Bye," Ally said, hanging up. She slammed the phone down on the counter and turned. She jumped back with a yelp at seeing Harrison so close behind her. "*The hell are you doing?*"

Harrison couldn't answer at first, his mind racing with what little he knew. He could barely feel the ache or the pins and needles that were devouring his legs. He had questions, worries, various demands all tumbling through his head and he was having trouble getting any of them into a coherent statement. Only one thing managed to bubble up to the surface and fell out of his mouth. "Where's Max?"

"In Oregon."

Harrison struggled to stay upright, fixing a glare on Ally. He towered over her and leaned in closer as he tried to adjust his balance, his mind racing with what might have happened. "You're lying. Ally tell me—"

A flame ignited between the two of them and Harrison jumped back, falling on the ground. His feet appreciated him no longer standing on them. Ally frowned as she looked down at him. She waited a moment before kneeling down to meet his eyes. "We're staying here, Harrison," she told him firmly. "For all we know, he's on his way here now and we need to be here when he shows up."

"You stay," he said. Max did not go missing. Max told his parents every time he was going anywhere and called if there was a change in plans. He didn't sneak away to travel across the country. If he was missing, something was very wrong. "If he does show up, call me. But he's not coming here and you know it."

Gently, Ally put a hand on his shoulder and gripped it tight. "You need to calm down and—"

"If you don't let me go, you're coming with me."

Ally did not let go. A moment later, they were both gone.

CHAPTER TWO

PANIC ALONE GOT them to Oregon. Locations flashed past as he jumped across the country more rapidly than he ever had before. It didn't matter that he'd barely eaten, that his body felt weak and still numb in parts, or that he had some-one else hanging onto him the whole way. He couldn't stop to enjoy the solitude of the forest, pop in to see if anything was playing in that one perpetually empty theatre in Neb-raska, or even stop at the little burger joint in the middle of nowhere.

Harrison regretted the last one the most.

Ally barely managed to catch him before he hit the cement of the parking garage, his body refusing to take any more. Spots flashed over Harrison's vision and his head swam. He knew he was shaking. He should have at least eaten the full bag of chips when he had the chance, not that it would have helped. At least they made it to Portland, but now that he was here he wasn't sure he could get them the rest of the way to... wherever they were going.

He breathed in deep and his vision went white for a moment, his head spinning so strongly that Harrison lost track of which direction was up. His stomach turned and he felt the bile in the back of his throat, mixed with lumps of potato chips, threatening to spill over. He didn't dare move, not wanting to bring on the wrath of his stomach along with whatever it was his head was trying to do to him.

Max. He shouldn't try to find Max. Max didn't want to see him anymore. Why was he trying to find someone who wanted nothing to do with him? He should be staying away. He shouldn't even be here. Far away. He should be far away.

"We're going to be in so much shit," Ally muttered. She tried to get him to his feet, but Harrison was shaking too badly to even sit up. He could hear her let out an irritated sigh before she lowered him back down to the ground. She looked out to the empty parking stalls around them, and then pulled out her phone. "You just can't help being a dumbass, can you? No way we weren't seen."

She wasn't wrong, Harrison knew, but all he could focus on right now was how solid the ground was as he felt like he was coming apart. He had not been remotely careful as they moved across the country. He had kept to his usual route, but he normally took it when there was much less daylight. Emma would be furious and H&B would want a word with him about possibly letting the secret out to the public, though that was the least of his concerns right now.

He needed to know where Max was. Even if Max wanted him out of his life, he needed to make sure he was okay. Missing was not normal for him and, even if they were no longer together, he still wanted to at least make sure there was nothing wrong. As soon as he was sure, he could let him go back to his life and he would stay away. That was all. He just needed to make sure he was all right.

Harrison rolled over onto his side and tried to push himself up, but he had no strength left. Ally put a hand on his shoulder to keep him down. Her eyes stayed on her screen, thumb dancing across it. "Stay down for a bit," Ally told him. "You haven't eaten in at least a day and you just... just stay down. I got this."

"I'm okay," he insisted, though he didn't try to move. His voice was weak and his throat scratched as he tried to speak. He wasn't tired, his heart still hammering in his chest, but there was darkness lingering at the edge of his vision. His hands wouldn't stop shaking and he was getting worried they might dissolve away if he wasn't careful. Ally's hand pressing his shoulder down and the ground under him kept him together as he tried to catch his breath.

He wasn't sure how long they stayed there. He heard cars drive past and slow down. Some people shouted and Ally shouted back at them, muttering about nosey people as they drove away. Harrison didn't move. Slowly, the shaking was finally subsiding and he felt a little stronger.

A car pulled up next to them and Ally got to her feet. "About damn time," she snapped as a door opened.

"The hell happened?" Ted. That was Ted.

"Harrison's a dumbass, what do you think? You bring anything?"

"Jaime's got it."

Harrison tried to push himself up, a head rush knocking him back down on his arms. The world dipped around him. There was something in front of him and he looked up. Jaime knelt in front of him with a cup in one hand and a bag of Jimmy John's in the other. "Thanks," he said, taking the coke first. She helped him sit up, keeping a hand firmly on his back and putting the bag in his lap.

"You're an idiot," Jaime told him. She looked tired, her dress shirt wrinkled like she had slept in it the night before. Her hair was longer than she usually kept it, now covering the tops of her ears and hanging close to her eyes. He still didn't know what H&B was having her do, but whatever it was he doubted they were paying her enough to leave her this stressed. On the other hand, she was the only one who might know what was going on.

"I've heard." He drank a little more before opening up the bag. The world kept moving around him, but Jaime felt solid. "Found Max?"

"Eat," Ally told him. She moved over to give Ted a place to sit. "We'll talk when you can stand again."

Harrison opened his mouth to protest, but the looks he got from all of them kept him quiet. He grudgingly opened the bag. The smell made his stomach lurch and suddenly there was nothing more important than devouring this sandwich as quickly as his body would allow.

He knew where they were, at least. This parking garage wasn't far from Max's house. He could walk from here to find out if Max was there, and he sometimes did so he could pick up something small for him on the way. From here, Harrison could get to Max's home, work, or anywhere else he might be hiding. If Max was hiding at all, and nothing bad had actually happened to him.

"So what happened?" Ally asked, taking a seat next to them on the concrete. She shot him a glare before she added, "You don't think Max is maybe rushing across the country to try and apologize in person for sending Harrison home early?"

Jaime shifted behind him. Harrison leaned forward, managing to keep up on his own and let Jaime move around until she was next to him. "H&B don't think so," she said, not meeting their eyes. "He was home this morning. And they can't get in touch with Jack or Mary either."

"Mary always picks up," Ted agreed.

"But that doesn't mean Max isn't still trying to—"

"He wouldn't," Harrison told them. Focus was returning and he was starting to feel a bit stronger with some food in him. "He can't afford the trip. And Max is not hitchhiking. It's Max." Harrison took a deep breath and looked around, trying to figure out exactly where they were. "What day is it?"

"Saturday," Ted said.

"Did he go to work?"

Ally and Jaime both grabbed his shoulder. "Don't you even think about it," Ally told him. "You're done for today."

Harrison's eyes went to Ted. "Did he?"

Ted shrugged. "They don't tell me shit. I just know out of everyone Adam was keeping track of, I'm the only one they can find. And I'm *definitely* not supposed to be leaving my flat right now. You're lucky they're so busy with Adam and that break out that they're not going to notice I came to pick you up."

"Break out?"

"What happened to Adam?" Ally asked.

Jaime shook her head. "We don't know," she said. "He's in critical, though. He already called in Emma and Gavin. I think they know something."

There was a rush of relief that went through Harrison at that. At the very least, Emma might be too distracted to know that they'd run across the country. That meant he could focus on what was important. "What break out?" he repeated louder.

"So Emma's already here?" Ally asked. "She could have given us a heads up."

"Or maybe she tried and you were already half way across the country," Ted said.

"Ted. Break out."

"What break out?"

"You said there was a break out."

"No I didn't."

"Who broke out, Ted?"

"I..." He hesitated, looking between them. He faltered only a moment longer before his shoulders dropped, scowling as he shook his head. "I said *nothing*, you hear me? I'm not even supposed to know, but... They moved Willow from New England to here and she got out last night."

Harrison's hand was in his pocket immediately, fishing out his phone. Max could get mad if he wanted, but he had to know that he was all right. There was barely any charge left in it, but it should be enough to at least make one call. Just long enough for Max to pick up.

"They moved Willow *here?*" Ally demanded, hand tightening on Harrison's shoulder. She glanced over to see what he was doing. "Harrison, what are you—"

"You said I should call him," Harrison snapped at her.

"I don't know what they were thinking," Ted said. "I don't even know why she was there. I just walked past the room a couple days ago and saw her. And then this morning they're sending me home and that whole hall's been shut down and it's half destroyed."

Harrison was barely listening for two long rings as Ted talked. Max picked up and relief rushed over him. And then he heard the quiet voice on the other end. "Hello?"

Harrison blinked at the phone. That wasn't Max. "Tara?"

"Harrison?"

"Why do you— is Max there?" he asked. Something sounded familiar in the background. "Where are you?"

Tara paused on the other end, and he could hear her moving. "The pool. Can you meet me?"

Ally shot him a glare, tightening her grip on his shoulder. "Don't even—"

Harrison pulled himself away and vanished.

CHAPTER THREE

HARRISON REALIZED THIS was a bad idea as soon as his feet hit the ground. He fell back into the lockers of the small staff room, sending a loud clang echoing loudly enough that anyone could hear. The smell of chlorine hit him in a wave and his head spun. Closing his eyes, he tried to ground himself and catch his breath. At least he didn't feel like throwing up. And at least he knew he made it to the right place.

It might not have been the safest place, technically, but he had not yet been caught appearing in the small corner behind the lockers. It gave him a fine view of the staff room, able to easily see if anyone else was there having lunch at the small table in the center of the room. Failing that, at least he could hear the old microwave. Right now, it was empty. And everything was very quiet for a public pool on a Saturday.

Tara. He had to find Tara. For some reason, Tara had Max's phone, and Max did not let anyone take his—

Two people appeared in the room and Harrison pressed his back against the wall, shrinking out of sight. A male and female in their mid-twenties looked around the room, looking much more annoyed than anything else. She glared into every corner while he went to the fridge. Harrison couldn't quite see their hands, but he was pretty sure they were supposed to be looking for the source of the metallic clattering that still echoed in the small room.

He had seen both of them before. Maya and Levi worked for H&B in a slightly different capacity than Emma. They were less interested in keeping an eye on H&B's test subjects than tracking down anyone who was causing problems and keeping things quiet. It wasn't until H&B that he had learned that many more had escaped in that initial breakout, all of them terrifyingly powerful and mute.

If they caught him here...

Harrison disappeared from his spot and appeared in the washroom attached to the staff room. Stepping slowly so that he wouldn't make too much noise on the tile, he pressed his ear to the door and tried to listen for anything that might let him know that people who could teleport and who didn't talk were gone. His head still spun, but he pushed back the nausea. He had to concentrate.

Harrison waited until he heard the door swing close outside and breathed a sigh of relief. He slid down to the ground, resting

his head against the cool wall as his stomach turned uncomfortably, and tried to figure out what was going on. He didn't need to
be running from H&B. They hadn't actually done anything that
was suspicious. They might have known what was going on.

"Harrison?"

The quiet voice in the darkness made him jump, smacking
his shoulder into the wall. He bit back a groan as the world wavered around him. His eyes searched the darkness, but he couldn't
see anything. One hand reached up and he turned on the light.

Crouched in the corner and watching him was Tara. Harrison knew her mostly as one of Max's best friends and the girl
next door. Her mousy brown hair hung loose around her shoulders and her brown eyes were wide as she inched forward around
the toilet. She didn't look ready to come out entirely yet, waiting for him to say something. Cupped in her hands was Max's
phone.

He felt like he was coaxing a scared kitten out of hiding.
"Tara, what are you—"

"How did you get in here?"

Harrison blinked. "I walked," he said. It was his default answer whenever anyone might have caught him, though he was
realizing how hollow it sounded now.

"You didn't open the door."

His head was too stuffed with cotton and the room was moving too much for him to come up with some excuse. "What are

you doing in here?" He kept his voice low, still listening for anyone else who might be outside. "Why do you have Max's phone?"

Tara shifted back toward the wall, pulling Max's phone in closer to her and tucking it in her pocket. Harrison watched it disappear before he let his attention drift back to Tara. She pursed her lips and opened her mouth once. Twice. And closed it again. She shrunk back further into the corner, keeping the toilet firmly between them.

Was she scared of him?

"Look," she said finally. "Can I ask you something? Honestly?"

"Is now really the time?"

"You can teleport, right?"

Harrison stared at her. His head was still fuzzy from the fatigue and it was only getting worse as the moments passed, but he was pretty sure he had just heard that. He'd never heard anyone ask anything so blunt and exact before, and didn't know what to do. He wasn't supposed to let anyone know, was supposed to lie if he had to and then let H&B deal with convincing them that they were wrong, but right now he didn't know how to process this. "What?"

"That's how you visit Max so much," she said, crawling out and getting to her feet. "You've been to visit him almost every month. I thought it was weird that he never had to go pick you up from the airport. And that you could afford to keep buying plane tickets."

"Plane tickets are—"

"And I saw you just show up on his front door in the middle of the night. I knew that was you. You didn't even walk up to the door, you just appeared."

"You must have—"

"And you just appeared in the bathroom."

He went quiet. That one, he couldn't argue.

Tara took a breath. "You can, can't you?"

The world was spinning. Or maybe it was crashing down around him. Sure, Tara was pretty observant, but he didn't think she had seen him enough to have come up with all of this. He thought he'd managed to cover his tracks well enough. Part of him wanted to know why she was looking out her window at Max's front door so late at night that she saw him.

She stood up now, stepping around the toilet and getting closer to him. "Because we need to get out of here before they get back, so now's not the time to pretend you don't have super powers."

"What?" This was all happening so fast, but he could see the desperation on her face. They should probably get out of here before they were found. They didn't want to be found by anyone here. It was somewhere that they shouldn't be.

"We have to go." She grabbed him by the forearm and tugged him away from the wall. "Now."

"Fine," Harrison said. He was already screwed so what was one more thing? They were gone before the door opened.

* * *

HARRISON LOST HIS footing as soon as he landed. He fell out of Tara's grasp and landed hard on the pavement. He felt queasy, but managed to keep the contents of his stomach inside of him. Barely. The world swam around him, though he was able to pick out the stunned faces of Ted, Ally, and Jaime around him as he let his head rest on the solid concrete to wait out the gentle earthquake that only he could feel.

"*What the hell, Harrison?* You are in so much shit, you know that?"

"Hey Tara," Ted said awkwardly. "What's up?"

"Oh my god," Tara said, looking around and backing away from all of them. "I... I'm... Oh my god..."

"You're gonna be okay," Ted tried to tell her, his hands out like he was trying to calm a particularly startled cat. He moved slowly closer, though he looked alarmed that he might actually get close enough to touch her. "Deep breaths. There's a perfectly reasonable explanation for all of this."

"Doesn't need to be," Jaime muttered, a frown on her face as she watched. For how everyone else was freaking out, she wasn't remotely bothered by Tara's appearance. She moved over to Harrison's side, helping him sit back up. She passed a look from Tara to Harrison and Ally, a finger dancing away from her head. "Static," she signed.

Ally's eyes shot over to Tara, followed slowly afterward by Harrison's. He had never noticed it before. He wasn't even sure if he was noticing it now, watching as Ted seemed to be coaxing her calmer. His head was swimming too much from how badly he'd overextended himself, but he couldn't remember a time that he'd been around Tara that there wasn't a little bit of static in the back of his head. Max had always been there, though, and that was just what happened when Max was there. It had never occurred to him that Tara might also...

He was too dizzy to put everything together, his stomach turning over again. He brought his knees up and rested his head between them. Slow breaths. Breathe. There was no rush. He just had to wait for the world to stop moving around him. No matter what happened now, he was in trouble with H&B. They would bring down whatever consequences they had for him regardless of how fast he ran, and he wasn't even capable of standing right now.

He had definitely pushed himself too far today. At least the ground was being good enough to stop moving so much. He should probably eat more at least. His body was aching for rest, though his mind was racing, remembering the phone in Tara's pocket and wondering if he'd find out what happened to Max before H&B caught him.

"Is he okay?" Tara's voice said, concern laced through it. He caught movement like she was coming closer, but she stopped. "I didn't think I was right."

"Someone just tell me what's going on," Ally said, sounding irritated. "If we're all getting in shit for breaking contract, I want to know what it's for, at least."

There was a pause before Tara finally spoke again, her voice timid and quiet. "I think I saw something," she said. "I was... I was going to meet Max after work and something happened. I'm not really sure what."

Ally scoffed, though no one paid any attention.

"The pool got evacuated." Her voice was stronger and the pace of her words started to pick up. "I kind of remember there being a leak, but that doesn't feel like it was right. I can kind of... There was a fight. I think there was a fight. And Max wasn't anywhere. So I went in to try and figure out where he was, but there were people inside. They were like that guy that Max has to talk to every once in a while. Adam? Like him. Didn't talk, all sign language. And I could remember hearing an ambulance, but I don't know what happened. But I know there was *something*, I just don't know what."

"How did you get in there?" Harrison asked, echoing her question from earlier. He tried to look up, but the rest of the world wasn't so kind as the ground, so kept staring at the pavement. Tara was starting to panic. He could feel it in that prickling of static that was starting to seep into his mind. Max had told him once that calming her down was as simple as repeating a question until she answered it.

"What?"

"How did you get in there?"

Tara understood what he was asking the second time around. Her voice went flat and sarcastic. The static lessened. "I walked."

"Give me your phone," Ted said, not unkind, but far too demanding. Harrison raised his head to watch her hand over Max's phone. Ted took it, slipping it into his pocket before extending his hand again. "No, *yours*," he said. "You have that on you?"

"Why?" she asked. Her hand was on her pocket. She definitely had it on her.

"Just let me see it," Ted insisted.

Ally hesitated before she unlocked it and handed it over, staying right at his side as he started pressing things on the screen. He couldn't see her face, but watched as her body went rigid as he seemed to find something on there. "Shit," Ted muttered. "What is this?"

"I don't remember that," Tara said, stricken. "I... What is that?"

"I think that's why Adam's in the hospital."

There was a scuffling, noise happening all at once as the rest went to crowd around the phone. Harrison raised his head, though already felt the rush come over him as soon as the movement happened. He tried to push past it, but his stomach was already turning, keeping him down. "What is it?"

"It's just..."

"It's Willow," Jaime told him, the frown on her face bleeding into her voice. She straightened up in an instant, jaw set and looking away from the phone to the sky behind them. "We need to find Mary and Jack."

"What about Max?"

"We know where Max is," Ally told him.

Harrison took in a shaky breath, the dread settling in the pit of his stomach. He wanted to throw up, but instead he let them help him into Ted's car. The glass was cool and solid, at least, and he rested his head against it as the rest of them piled in. He'd see the whatever it was they watched when everything stopped moving, though part of him dreaded what was on Tara's phone.

CHAPTER FOUR

THEY DROPPED TARA off, Harrison observing as Jaime handed her a card with her name and H&B's logo on it. Neither of them said a word about it, nor did anyone else in the car, and he was too tired to ask. He wasn't quite sure what Jaime did for H&B that she would have business cards. Right now it didn't matter.

He couldn't help staring at Max's house next door as they drove off again. He wanted to believe that everything was fine. H&B would handle this. Sure, they seemed to be torturing Max every time they brought him in for testing, but they didn't want anything bad to happen to him. They could find him and get him back.

That was until he saw the video.

He'd handed over his phone so Ted could charge it as they drove. He got Ted's phone exchange so he could see what they had. Ally didn't look happy about it, but she was still mad about being dragged across the country. Jaime sat next to him and he could feel her eyes watching him and not the screen as he hit play.

There was no sound, but there didn't need to be. Even from across the parking lot, even dressed in plain clothes, he recognized Willow just fine. There was already a lot of red on the scene, and it looked like most of it was from the other man. Adam stood back from her, though he was only upright for a moment. He fell forward and collapsed into a puddle of red on the ground.

There was a movement at the door and Harrison saw him. That splash of red hair with the green shirt he wore for work. He didn't know how long Max had been standing there, but he was trying now to get back inside, the door pulled open but his feet not able to move him into the building.

And then Willow moved. It wasn't until she moved that he realized the horror that must have just taken place. Dropping from her hand was an arm — Adam's. She wasn't anywhere near it when it hit the ground, tossing it aside like it was nothing now that she had Max in her sights.

In one fell swoop, she grabbed onto him and vanished into thin air, the camera now flailing around to see a small group of people watching and freaking out as they tried to make sense of what they'd seen.

It was a short video, but it felt like it had gone on forever. Harrison played it again, feeling ill as he realized just how much blood must have been on the ground just outside. They had probably evacuated the place. It explained why Levi and Maya were there too. If you wanted people to forget what they saw, those two knew how to do it.

Out of everything that happened in the video, the thing that bothered him the most was Willow. She wasn't supposed to be here. There was no reason for them to move her out here. The last time Harrison had heard, she was unresponsive, but now he watched her clearly mobile, just finished spilling enough of Adam's blood that Harrison wasn't sure he would make it, and taking Max away.

Willow taking him wasn't that surprising when he thought about it. He had been there at the end, and had blamed himself for what happened to her. Harrison had told him enough times that they didn't deserve his sympathy after everything they had done to him and were planning to do to the rest of them, but it seemed Willow didn't agree. Even if she didn't remember that, she didn't much like Max before it.

Harrison barely noticed the quiet that had fallen over the car until Ally spoke. Her words came out nervous and uncertain, her eyes firmly on the road ahead. "So, how's Jack? And Mary."

Oh. Right. She hadn't seen Jack in quite a while.

"Fine," Ted told her, completely missing her unease as he drove. "Or I hope they're fine. Mary usually picks up."

"Good," Ally said. She shifted in her seat, her shoulders tight and holding her arms close to her. "Good..."

"He's not mad," Harrison offered. His head didn't leave the cool glass and watched as they turned into downtown. At least, Jack had said he wasn't mad about it. "He gets it. I mean, he's not happy about it, but he gets it. I think Mary is more pissed than he is. Just try not to bring it up."

"Bring what up?" Ted asked.

"Ally set Jack on fire the last time she saw him," Harrison said.

"You *what?*"

"I didn't..."

Her protest died off as soon as she ran out of words, Ally looking very firmly out the window and avoiding the glances from Ted. Her face was hidden by her hair, but Harrison figured she was probably turning a shade of red.

"It was before you," Harrison said. "Jack and Mary, they left initially and then Jack came back to try and get us out of there. Apparently Mary told him it was a bad idea, but he did it anyway. And with Luke around, we thought he was one of the guys in suits coming back for us. I think I broke his jaw first, and then Ally set him on fire."

His tone covered how bad he still felt about the whole thing. It had been a while since he and Jack had reconciled what happened, but just looking at him was enough to bring the shame of it back. Jack didn't like to talk about it anymore than Harrison, but once he was sure Harrison wasn't going to try and hit him again he was fine. They talked about what happened only once, about Luke and Willow and how badly they had gotten in their heads. How it wasn't either of their faults. And then they never talked about it again and quietly agreed to treat it like it never happened.

"You actually stuck around long enough to throw a punch?" Ted laughed, a grin tugging at the side of his mouth. "Ally I can believe. You hanging around long enough... Luke really must have done a number on us. It's okay, though," Ted added, nudging Ally with his elbow. She didn't move away. "Jack's never mentioned anything, so he can't be that mad about the whole thing still. And it's not like you're going to do it again, right?"

Ally didn't say anything and an uncomfortable quiet settled over the car. Ted at least knew not to press any further, but Harrison was thinking about that day. There was a time it was difficult to remember. Even after, it wasn't until Harrison had talked to Mary and seen Jack that he knew just how wrong they had been.

At the time, he thought it was just one of the men in suits coming to take them away. They didn't know how he'd found them or how he'd gotten in, but they knew he was dangerous.

And they had to do what they could to defend themselves. They had seen how dangerous they were first hand plenty of times, seen how much trouble they gave Luke and Willow. It made perfect sense at the time.

After that, Jaime had been the one to point out that it was Jack that they had tried to burn alive in a stranger's living room. And they had somehow rationalized it away as him going to the other side. It was amazing that Jack was willing to associate with them at all. Harrison was certain he would have cut all ties with them after that.

Jack and Mary lived together in an apartment close to the school in the middle of downtown. Both attended only part time, working the rest of the time at H&B. Harrison didn't ask how Mary managed to convince her parents, deciding that he was much better off not knowing what convinced her very conservative parents to let her move in with her boyfriend. He also didn't ask how she managed to negotiate rent at half the cost of any other unit in the building. He suspected she used the same method both times, having learned it from Max, and that H&B had let it slide.

Harrison could at least stand on his own two feet and walk on his own with only a little wavering when they got out of the car. Jaime stayed close by his side, ready to catch him, and they made their way to the door. Ted frowned as they got close, looking around. "How are we getting in?"

"Buzz?" Harrison suggested as they got to the door. He dialed 312 into the panel by the door and waited. It rang several times, but no one picked up.

"Might not be home?" Ally suggested.

"And not picking up?" Ted asked, growing more concerned. "Something's weird here. Can... Where's Jaime?"

Harrison blinked, his eyes darting around until he spotted her on the other side of the glass doors of the building. She swung them open, nodding for them to follow her to the elevators.

"How did you get in here?" Harrison asked.

"Come on," Jaime said. "Ted's right. Something's wrong here."

Harrison fell to the back of the line, not only because he was still shaky on his feet. Something was definitely wrong here, but Mary not picking up the phone wasn't the only thing. Jaime had definitely gotten into the doors without a key. She had opened them from the inside. His mind was struggling to work, trying to remember if she had ever done anything like that before. H&B did ask them to do strange things in tests from time to time, but they never worked. No matter what they tried, Harrison couldn't set anything on fire and Ally was never able to make the ground shake. But maybe one of them had been able to do something.

But that wasn't why they were here. They approached the door and collectively realized that they didn't have any way to get in if there was no one home. Well, Harrison did, but the way Ally looked at him with that warning look made him wonder if she knew he felt like he was only barely managing to keep himself together. He hoped they were home.

Or maybe Jaime could do that trick with the door again. She had to have done something.

Ted knocked and the door swung open. "They didn't even close it properly," he said, glancing back at Harrison. It was an older building and the doors didn't always close properly, but it was strange that they would leave it unlocked like this, even if they were home. Even if they could probably deal with intruders, they were a bit too private to just let anyone who wanted to wander in. It felt wrong, but Ted held the door open anyway to let them in.

Most of the place looked fairly normal. There were papers scattered on the tables and counters and a laptop on the coffee table. A few dishes sat on top of a small stack of books by the couch. A stack of bottles lay in a mess by the bathroom door, overflowing the box meant to contain them. It looked mostly normal in here, except for the cracked television and the slightly ajar door to their bedroom. He had only been to this place twice before, but he remembered no crack in the television.

"That's weird," Ted muttered, going for the bedroom door. "They don't leave this open. Like, ever." He was across the room at the bit of strangeness in a moment, freezing at the door. Harrison watched as his body went rigid for a moment, then he slowly stepped back. He looked pale. The last time he'd seen that expression on Ted's face, he'd just watched a video of Adam getting his arm ripped off and Max getting taken. "We need to... Jaime, call H&B."

They were all in the doorway a moment later, taking in the scene. The place had been completely trashed. The closet door was cracked and falling off the hinges, the dresser knocked aside. The mirror had shattered and glass littered the carpet. There was a hole in the drywall. Over everything, there was the smell and sight of blood sprinkled across the room and in streaks on the carpet.

"What happened?" Ally asked, staring at it and wandering into the room, eyes wide and trying to understand what she was seeing.

Ted grabbed her before she could go too far. "It's basically a crime scene, Ally."

"But..." She stopped at the sound of something else in there with them. Ted managed to block the rest of them from getting in, but it was clear they weren't alone in here. Something had definitely moved somewhere. They had heard a sound that was like scratching, but also very much not.

And again.

"Do they have a cat?" Ally asked, her voice very low.

"Their lease doesn't allow it," Jaime said.

Ted hesitated before he stepped around Ally and into the room, arm covering his mouth so he didn't have to smell the blood. Everything was still fresh. So fresh. Harrison stepped forward, leaning on Ally and trying to keep it from making him throw up what little he had inside of him. The smell of it was dizzying and they watched as Ted went timidly into the room. Jaime followed him. No one made a sound.

Scratch.

"Bed," Jaime said, moving toward it.

Ted was closer and dropped to the ground to look under it. He balked at the sight of it, covering his mouth firmly with his hand and fighting a gag. Jaime knelt down next to him to take a look, jaw set and frowning at whatever she was seeing. She reached a hand underneath it and a moment later, Ted jumped.

"Oh thank god," he breathed, getting back to his feet. "We gotta move the bed."

"We've got this," Ally told Harrison, pressing him back against the wall and out of her way. She let her hand stay on his chest for a moment and looked at him, silently telling him to stay put before she joined them at the bed. She didn't look at what was under there, instead bending down to get a grip the bottom of the bed frame.

Harrison stayed at the door, wanting to protest but knowing that he couldn't do anything to help. He was still dizzy and exhausted and only wanted to sleep, through the fear and adrenaline pumping through his body kept him up. He felt useless, but even the smell of the blood was making him dizzy and he wasn't sure his body could handle lifting anything right now.

Jaime stepped back, already on her phone. Ally and Ted lifted the bed, tipping it over onto its side and sending it crashing into the wall. Ally stared at what was under there for only a moment before she ran out past Harrison to the washroom. Ted knelt down, giving Harrison a fine view of just what was under there.

Jack laid there, bleach blond hair covering his face. He was bloody and broken on the ground, though at least it didn't look like the blood was pooling around him. It was hard to tell for certain. His breath came in scratching, desperate gasps. He let his head fall to one side, green eyes half lidded and looking up at the people around him. The corner of his mouth twitched, jaw relaxing like he was about to say something, but only another ragged breath escaped him.

"Ambulance is on the way," Jaime said, pocketing her phone.

"What happened?" Ted asked softly. "Jack?"

Jack managed another ragged breath and tried to sit up. He groaned and fell back to the ground, curling into a ball and stopping part way. Ally and Ted stepped closer, Ted bending down to actually check if he was all right. A low growl escaped him when Ted got close. "What the fuck is happening?"

CHAPTER FIVE

JACK WOULD BE fine, they insisted. He was half conscious when they loaded him into the ambulance, and the police did not want to talk to them as they went to close off the scene of the break in. It seemed strange at first, but then he saw Levi in the lobby. He didn't know where Maya was, but H&B clearly had their hands in this already. Harrison stayed out of the way and got in the car with Ted to follow the ambulance.

Harrison wasn't a fan of hospitals. He hadn't had to deal with them often in his life, but the times he had involved him sitting in the waiting room and hoping for good news. Even though it usually was, no amount of good news helped that dread in the pit of his stomach or the cold that ran up his back as he waited. He felt helpless and only his need to know for sure kept him from getting the hell out of there.

No one spoke, leaving Harrison's thoughts free to roam just to where he didn't want them to. He wasn't sure why he was here. He'd run across the country worried about a boy that didn't want to see him anymore. Max had told him specifically to forget all about him, and here he was. He had never had this kind of trouble after a break up before. He'd been good about giving people space, about letting them move on with their lives while he got on with his own.

"This was a mistake," he muttered, not looking at Ally sitting next to him. "I'm sorry I dragged you into this."

"Damn well better be," she told him. "How are you holding up?"

"Still dizzy." They stopped for more food on the way over, but nothing was sitting well, and his head was spinning for too many reasons. "This was a mistake."

"Popping across the country and nearly killing yourself over a guy who broke up with you? Yeah, not the brightest thing you've ever done."

"You know he didn't mean to," Ted told her. "Testing just screws him up really badly. Max barely has control over what he's doing after a day in there."

Part of Harrison knew Ted was right. Max turned into a very different person when he was in there. He was so scared, so distant, so unlike himself. But still, those words echoed in his head and it felt like he meant it. "He said he didn't want to see me again."

Ally shifted a little closer to him. "Might not be the worst thing."

"Is now really the best time for this?" Ted shot back at her.

"I like Max, but this isn't exactly the first time he's done this," Ally said. "It's not like I'm saying I don't want to make sure he's okay. I'm still worried about what's happening, but this is separate. And it's becoming a pattern. I shouldn't have to—"

"If you don't stop, I will knock this whole building down!" Jack's voice roared from inside his hospital room. A string of profanity followed it, growing quieter as a second voice insisted that he let her do her job and not so gently reminded him that this was a hospital and he would be murdering a lot of people if he tried to do just about anything right now.

Ally went rigid at the sound of Jack's voice, her eyes wide on the door. Whatever she was going to say was forgotten and she looked like she might never move again.

Ted cracked a smile at the sight of her. "Jack sounds better," he said. "You want to go say hi?"

Another angry string of profanities came out of the room and Ally stayed very still. "I think that can wait," she said.

"It'll be fine," Ted insisted, a laugh behind his words. "So long as you don't mention your theories on Max, I'm sure you guys will make up just fine."

"Just don't mention it," Jaime agreed. "He knows your brains were messed up."

Harrison couldn't place that look on her face. She was scared, yes, but there was something else on there too. Something like betrayal or disbelief flickered through her expression before she looked to back to the room, watching the door as it fell suddenly completely silent in there. Emma walked out of the room, letting the door shut behind her before any of them could get a glimpse of what was happening inside.

Emma had changed a lot in the last year. She was still strangely pale, but now dressed much more like an average professional who might actually have a full time job with a company like H&B. Her red eyes were still strange to meet for a long time, but he'd gotten used to that feeling that she could tell all of his secrets just from looking at him. Now, the unease was from the fact that he'd done something that she had to deal with.

Now those eyes were bloodshot and she looked exhausted. The circles were dark on her pale skin, and her feet lingered close to the ground as she walked. She pinched her eyes shut for a moment before opening them wide and looking around at the group of them.

"Hey," Harrison signed at her. "What are you doing here?" He spoke the words as well out of habit, even though he really didn't have to do both. Emma could hear just fine, as could the rest, but it felt strange to speak back to someone who was signing.

"Adam's awake," she told them, her fingers not as sharp as they usually were. "He said you were here, Harrison. He wanted to talk to you."

Harrison hesitated, looking back to Ally and Ted and Jaime before he spoke, not getting up. "Isn't he missing an arm?"

Ally smacked him hard in the arm for that, but Emma only smiled. "He's managing," she said, before confusion crossed her face. "How did you know?"

Harrison shrugged and got to his feet, making a careful note that he was probably not supposed to know that. He had just popped across the country and hadn't been there when Adam was attacked outside of the pool. As far as she knew, he hadn't been anywhere near the pool. She probably didn't know about the video, and he definitely didn't want to drag Tara into the middle of this. He still didn't know what H&B was doing, but he wasn't ready to trust that they were doing the right thing yet. They were the ones who had brought Willow here in the first place, and none of them had so much as mentioned Max yet. "Where's Adam?" he asked instead.

Emma was clearly aware that he was avoiding the subject, but she was much too tired to do anything about it. She pressed her fingers into one of her eyes and stifled a yawn before waving for them to follow her. They went down the hall, to a very different waiting room. It smelled sterile and it lacked the sounds of anyone protesting their treatment or sound at all besides the gentle beep and hum of machines. It felt hushed and sombre, like when they weren't sure if Jaime was going to make it last year.

The room was open and they trickled in, finding Gavin passed out in a chair in the corner. On his lap was a notebook with several things written in it, pen still in hand as he dozed. Shaking her head, Emma grabbed a blanket from outside to drape over him as the rest found a spot around the walls to stand. It was not large enough for this many people, but none of them wanted to stay back.

The sight of Adam made Harrison falter. His face had been cleaned up, though there was a long scratch that ran from above his eye and down his neck that was held closed with small bandages. His eyes were closed and he wasn't moving, but Harrison was careful to note the gentle rise and fall of his chest. His arm was missing and the socket had been completely bandaged, though there was still the acrid scent of blood and burning lingering in the air. Something about him just seemed so fragile, like a whisper of his old self. A drip went into his remaining arm, and the monitor pulsed steadily, the beeping steady if quiet.

Gently, Emma went next to Adam and poked his cheek. His head lolled to one side before he snapped up, red eyes looking around alert and body rigid. He winced, a groan escaping him and Harrison carefully avoided looking at his mouth and the distinct lack of tongue inside of it until he shut his lips again. He relaxed back into the pillows. Irritated and tired, he looked around at them. He didn't move at first, but a frown grew across his face soon after. His eyes went down to where his left arm used to be, then over to at Emma.

"He says hi," she signed for them.

Irritation flashed across the fatigue on Adam's face, Adam making no attempt to look remotely pleasant. Harrison got the feeling that he was trying to say quite a bit that Emma wasn't getting across, though there was some comfort in seeing him frown. If he could manage to be annoyed, then maybe he wasn't doing as badly as the silence seemed to imply. His eyes went back to Gavin in the corner, narrowing sharply for a moment before he turned back to look at the rest of them.

Silence hung in the air for a long moment, a haze of irritated static growing in their heads. Adam moved his remaining hand, the movements small and jerking as he tried to sign. "Sorry," he said, pulling back on the static and taking a breath. He looked no less irritated, but the haze over their minds started to lighten.

A tone bleeped in the quiet of the room. Jaime pulled her phone out of her pocket and left the room without another word.

"It's okay," Ally said, her voice quiet as she inched a little further away from his bed. "What happened?"

Gavin stirred in the corner, though he looked like he could use another day's worth of sleep. He started at the sight of so many people in the room, looking from them to Adam and back again. He didn't seem to recognize any of them, or at least didn't care who any of them were before he looked back at Adam.

"Where the hell is the doctor?" he asked, his movements sharp and his face irritated.

Adam didn't move in the bed or make a sound, but Gavin could still hear him. "Already? You should have— I'm *fine*."

"If you're fine," Emma cut in, "can you go make sure Jack doesn't try to bring the roof down on all of us?"

"Did they find Jack?" he asked. "Where the hell was he?"

"In his apartment. No Mary."

Harrison didn't know why that was significant, but everything seemed much more serious with the revelation that they didn't have Mary with them. Gavin's frown turned into a scowl and he shook his head, his hands moving furiously.

"He's not my problem," Gavin insisted. "I have enough to do with all this."

"Not for another hour," Jaime told him. Harrison didn't know when she'd gotten back in the room, but she was standing next to him now. "But we are going to have to go."

Adam reached with his remaining hand and grabbed Gavin's forearm. Gavin stiffened at first, glaring back at Adam's stern gaze before he finally relaxed. He put one hand on Adam's before he got to his feet "Fine," he said. "Ted, you come with. When I leave, you're in charge of making sure the hothead doesn't try to knock the hospital down."

"I have no idea what's going on," Ally muttered as they left the room.

With half of them gone, Emma dropped into the chair and looked like she was about to take a nap until Adam dropped his hand on her head and started tapping. The static in the air around them grew and Harrison could feel it creeping up into the back of his mind, though Adam didn't seem to care. Emma glowered back at him, but his hand moved in one short motion. "Now," he said.

Emma didn't look pleased, but she sat up in the chair and looked at the pair of them as her hands started to move. "He says don't go after them. H&B have this. Adam wasn't expecting it and he got surprised, but we got this now. If you start trying to get involved, you're going to get in the way and nothing will be resolved. We'll find both of them a lot easier if you all just stay out of the way."

As comfortable as Harrison had grown around Emma, there was a reason he never quite trusted her. She was much too comfortable with just doing what H&B told her to do, even if that was lying to them and keeping them in the dark about what was going on. It didn't escape him that she had said nothing about what was going on. He wanted more answers than platitudes, and he wanted to know what had happened.

"You took your time finding Jack, and he was in his own apartment," Ally pointed out.

"We were looking into a few other matters," Emma told her. "We have this under control."

"Willow took both of them, didn't she?" Harrison asked, already knowing the answer. He ignored the surprise on Emma's face, focusing on Adam. "What was she even doing here?"

"None of your concern," Emma said instead. "We have it under control, but I'm sure if you know that, then you understand why the five of you need to keep a bit of a low profile for a while."

He glanced back to Adam, watching his expression sour more as Emma continued. He reached out and rapped his knuckles hard on her head to get her attention, but she ignored him.

"Except that she left Jack behind," Harrison said. "Does she even want the rest of us? Why is she even here?"

Emma tried to answer, but her hands fell to her lap and stayed there. She shot a glare at Adam as she tried to pull her arms back, but they wouldn't move.

Pain crossed Adam's face as he tried to sign something, the static growing thicker in the air and in Harrison's ears. Despite how heavy it was in his head, it seemed to make the jerky, stilted movements of Adam's hand make more sense.

"Watch Jack and keep him out of this," he told them. "She is right, you should stay out of this. I don't know why they brought Willow here, but there's something strange about all of this. She shouldn't have been able to find anyone, but if she found them, then she'll be able to find all of you as well. She's after something specific and this has something to do with—"

Emma's hand shot out and grabbed his, pushing it down to the bed. Anger filled his face as the static grew angrier in their minds, but Emma was much too late already. They both knew exactly what he was trying to warn them about without having to make a gesture.

Luke.

"But he's..." Ally's words died on her lips, not sure how to continue.

Harrison was already out of the room and heading down the hall. This wasn't happening. Luke was dead and Willow was supposed to be as good as gone as well. This was supposed to be over, and if H&B couldn't figure out how to fix this, then he was going to just have to do this himself. If he was fast enough, he probably wouldn't have to even deal with Willow.

Half a plan was forming in his mind, most of it consisting of finding Max and dragging him out of there before Willow had the chance to do anything to him. He'd get Mary out of there as well, though he still didn't know what Willow could want with her. H&B could deal with her however they wanted.

And Max...

Well, once he was out, he would let Max decide whether or not he wanted to see him again. For right now, he just needed to figure out where Willow had taken him.

A hand grabbed his shoulder and Harrison jumped, pulling himself back and spinning around. Maya stood behind him, a gentle smile on her face and red eyes watching him carefully as her hands started to move. "Harrison, right?" she asked. "You're going to need to come with me."

"Why?"

"Well, you did leave your testing session a few days early," she pointed out. "And, given the circumstances, H&B has determined that it's better if we keep you all in one place, just to be safe. What do you know about what's happening?"

"Willow," Harrison told her.

Maya looked almost pleased that he knew. "Yeah, the psycho is back. And she doesn't have her boyfriend around to make her pull her punches."

"You think Willow is going to come for the rest of us?" he asked.

"If she does, won't it be better to be somewhere with a good amount of backup?" Maya laughed and urged him to follow her. "H&B will make sure none of you get hurt while you're under their roof. Come on, your room is waiting."

CHAPTER SIX

WHILE TED WAS running Ally's session, Harrison was partnered with Kenzie. She normally worked with Max, and Harrison had often joked about how he attracted pretty blondes. She was normally fairly upbeat and chatty, but today she stuck very strictly to the routine of the tests, eyes going back to the papers in front of her frequently and reading them over and over until she was sure of what she was doing.

Despite working for H&B, Kenzie was one of them. Like Ally, she could set things on fire with her mind, but she was not nearly so precise about it. When she got particularly flustered, Harrison had seen her catch the ends of her hair on fire. For the moment, he was keeping his nose alert in case anything smelled of burning.

"Okay," she said, tucking the papers under one arm and hooking her other in his. "Last thing. You need to try and pop into that one with me."

Across the small room were a series of closets with doors that only opened from the outside, though Harrison didn't know why. He'd been asked to go in them several times, often holding things that were much too large for the room. He usually dropped whatever it was he was carrying on the way over like it was something that was too large to fit through the door, except there was no door. He wasn't quite sure how it worked, only that this was a terrible idea. Kenzie pointed at the one in the middle, one he knew for certain was barely big enough for him.

"You aren't going to fit," he told her.

"Well, maybe if you lost a few pounds we could both make it in there." She smiled back at him and didn't let go. "Come on, you've carried a lot of other things in there. Do the same with me, and then we can all go home."

Harrison let out a hollow laugh.

"What?" Kenzie asked.

Harrison shook his head and did as he was asked. They appeared in one of the small rooms and Harrison immediately regretted it. They were painfully crammed in, limbs tangled together and jamming into one another. He never wanted to be this close to another woman. His arms were bent back and her knee found the spot between his ribs and stomach.

Harrison pushed himself back and disappeared from the one room, appearing into the main room where he could breathe. A shiver ran up his spine, not liking the feeling of just how cramped and tangled he'd felt. "I told you!" he snapped back at her. "We don't both fit in there!"

"We did for a second!" Kenzie called back. "Hey Harrison? How do I get out of here?"

Harrison looked at the room that Kenzie was now trapped in and stopped. He looked left, and right, counting the doors and realizing that it hadn't been the one he was trying to get into. This was much too far to the right. Had he missed? *Could* he miss?

"Hey Harrison?" Kenzie asked again. "How do I get out of here?"

Harrison let out a breath and tried to focus. A doorknob on the inside, now that he thought about it, would have made this trial much worse. When he opened the door, Kenzie had a flame cradled in her hand that was already the size of her head. Her brown eyes were wide when they met his. "Have you tried the door?" he asked. "You know, before you try burning down the place."

Her wonder and fear turned to a frown. "Very funny."

"You were in there for three seconds."

"*I* can't get out!"

Harrison held his hands up in surrender, the smile on his face holding back a laugh. She brushed past him to a desk, shuffling through her papers to take her notes. He leaned over her shoulder, seeing that all she was actually noting down this whole time was whether or not he could actually do any of these experiments, not what the results actually were.

"They're going to ask me to do that again, aren't they?" he asked.

Kenzie nodded, not caring that he was looking. "They're not going to ask me to actually conduct the full tests on my own. I don't have a degree for that."

"If you did, then you wouldn't have had to get shoved into the closet. You could get some poor intern to do that for you."

"*I'm* the poor intern." She finished and closed the folder, setting her pen down on top of it. "But maybe they'll send you back so I don't have to do that again. Why are you still here, anyway? I thought you got out of here when Max started losing it."

Harrison stared at her, brows knitting in confusion as she turned back.

"What?" she asked.

"Didn't someone tell you what's going on?" Harrison asked. She worked for them. It was strange that she didn't seem to know.

Kenzie hesitated and looked distinctly smaller. She didn't meet his eyes, looking at just about everything else. Harrison could smell the start of something smoking. "I generally know what happened in the east wing?" she offered weakly.

"Willow broke out."

"Oh good, you already know she was here." She looked genuinely relieved at that. The smell of smoke tapered off. "That was... no one was supposed to know about that. I only found out by accident. How did you find out?"

"She kidnapped Max," Harrison told her. "And put Adam in the hospital. And Jack. And... I don't know what's going on with Mary, but it probably also has to do with her."

"Oh," Kenzie said. She toyed with the collar of her shirt, shifting away from him and looking back at the door. It was clear that no one had told her about any of this. She pursed her lips to let out a long, slow breath as her mind worked to try and put all of this in order.

And then that breath stopped along with the rest of her. She looked up suddenly and met his eyes. "Oh..."

"Oh?" Harrison repeated.

"It was..." She glanced at the door before she continued, her voice a whisper. "Like, at the very end of it. Max was— he never does well in these things. But he was worse a lot faster this time. Which, I mean, he gets worse faster every time. That's not that weird. But I heard someone say that at the end, Willow could walk. And that she was starting to, like, move. Not normally, I'm guessing, but she didn't do that before, right?"

"Why are we whispering?" Harrison asked, looking back at the door as well. He wasn't sure which part of this he was most concerned about. The secrecy, that Willow was moving, or that Max was apparently even worse after he left.

"The boss is in," she told him. "Doctor Gethen. They called him in after Willow broke out, but he's supposed to be getting in today."

Harrison frowned. So they were bringing the higher ups at H&B to deal with this. Doctor Gethen was head of research, meaning he was in charge of all the test subjects, and the one who insisted that they keep torturing Max the way they did. "And I'm not supposed to know about this?"

"*I'm* not supposed to know about this!" she hissed back. "And I can't afford to lose this job! But, like, they never told me Max was *gone*. Who'd want to hurt him? I mean, I don't really even know who Willow is, honestly..."

"You..." Harrison started, though he wasn't sure what to do with any of this. He supposed Max was rarely in a good enough condition to chat, and he didn't like bringing up what had happened, but Jack or Mary might have mentioned something when they were in. Ted worked in the same capacity as she did and he should have definitely brought it up. "You need to talk to Ted more often. It's weird that he didn't tell you about all this."

"Max's friend? I don't usually have shifts with him."

"You—"

The door opened and Kenzie jumped. While she busied herself with the notes, Harrison turned back to the door to see

Gethen looking in. He was a large man, much larger than he expected anyone who held a desk job to be. He might have been a bouncer at a particularly rough club at some point in the past and Harrison would not be surprised. The round, thick rimmed glasses did a decent job of getting people to mostly overlook him, but when he looked you over, those piercing blue eyes didn't regard you as human so much as a problem or an experiment.

Harrison had sat with him giving his story a long time ago, and after a while he started to notice the small scars that lined his skin. Small lines were etched into his face and fell across his hands, snaking up under his sleeves. There was something about him, how he looked at you and how he knew much more about your potential than you did. It was unsettling and Harrison wanted no part of it.

"Mr. Owens," he said, looking the pair of them over and settling on Harrison. "I need you to come with me."

He said a brief goodbye to Kenzie and she wouldn't even look up from her notes. Harrison could smell the faint scent of smoke and decided it was best to get out of there before her boss saw her hair catch fire.

Harrison walked down the hall one step behind Gethen. He wanted to ask what he wanted. Coming directly to get Harrison instead of sending a runner of some sort was strange and Harrison didn't trust it. Still, any questions he might have wanted to ask did not make it past his lips.

"You want to know why I came for you myself," he said. Harrison wasn't entirely unfamiliar to people reading his mind, but it was unsettling when there wasn't an aura of static around them. He didn't think Gethen could do anything, but he was never entirely certain. "We are looking to use all of the resources available to try and find Willow."

Harrison stayed quiet. He was hardly a resource. He didn't know what he thought Gethen was expecting him to know. He certainly wasn't about to start offering information that might accidentally incriminate himself.

"You're much quieter than the last time we spoke," he noted.

"Testing is tiring."

Gethen let out a small, sharp laugh. "I assure you, it could be much worse. But you all get to go back to your normal lives after, so we can't go too hard on you."

They walked in silence through the facility. Harrison wasn't sure if there were actually eyes on them as they walked or if he was just imagining it, but it felt like something was happening. It seemed quieter with him here, like people were on their best behaviour. Well, most people, at least.

As they came close to his office, Gethen spoke again. "Is there anything you would like to tell me?" he asked. His voice was calm and conversational, but Harrison couldn't help but feel like it was a threat.

"I just got back to this coast," Harrison told him. "I don't know anything about what happened."

Gethen nodded. "She is a very promising resource," he said. "Interesting. It would be a shame if we lost her. Both of them, really."

Gethen opened the door to his office and let Harrison in first. It was largely unused, Gethen normally working out of New England, and he could smell the musk from the curtains covering the windows. Someone had bothered to dust, at least, and neither the metal filing cabinets along one wall or the mess of screens along the other had any sign of dust on them. Only a couple of the screens were on, showing security footage from the front office of the building and one of the labs, but Harrison was suddenly acutely aware of every security camera that must be in the building. He wondered if the video came with audio as well.

Near the back of the room, there was a large oak desk with a computer sitting on top of it. In front were two chairs, one of them occupied by a motionless woman. Harrison took the empty seat next to her while Doctor Gethen went behind the desk.

Harrison knew Devlyn on sight, though he had only actually met her once. Where most of the Keepers tried to blend in, she had decided that was not her style. She dressed in bold red to match her eyes and streaked her hair with brilliant blue. A dark tattoo ran up her arm, thorns growing from a band around her wrist. She had smiled when she noticed him staring and told him that she'd recommend her guy when he wanted one.

She wasn't smiling now.

Gethen stayed standing as he rummaged through his drawers before pulling out a pad of paper with notes scrawled onto it. He looked carefully between the two of them before he nodded. "We'll make this quick. I'm going to ask a few things and she will make sure you stay honest. Understand?"

Harrison nodded, looking back over at Devlyn. She turned to look at him, her red eyes looking entirely lifeless. He shifted uncomfortably under her gaze, feeling the static starting to fill his mind. He scratched his ear, but took a breath. If he was cooperative it would be over sooner. It should only be a few questions and he had nothing to hide.

He wondered if that was one of his own thoughts, or one of hers.

Gethen looked at his notes as he spoke, his pen moving across the page. "Have you had any contact with Willow?" he asked.

"Not since last year," Harrison said.

"Did you know that Willow was here?"

"Not until after I came back."

"Why did you come back here, then?"

Harrison blinked slowly. The static was starting to make it hard to hear. His brain felt heavy in his head and his ears were filling with a tingling sensation. His hand rubbed the back of his neck, his pinky pressing into the base of his skull. It was getting harder to concentrate.

But he had to answer. If he answered, this would be over sooner. "Because Jaime called," he said. His words felt slow, but he couldn't make them come out any faster. "She said Max was missing. I had to come back."

"No you didn't," Gethen said, more to himself than Harrison. He made a note and gestured at Devlyn. The static started to lessen in his mind and Gethen looked over at her, studying her. "She's always been a little eager with that. Handy, but this is hardly the time for it. Now, how did you know where to find Mr. Cravesk?"

Harrison could almost think again. At least enough to recognize a stupid question. "In his apartment?" he asked.

Gethen pursed his lips and made a small hum before he put his pen to the page and made a note. "And do you have any way of finding Max yourself?" he asked. "Think hard. Has he developed some other way of contacting you yet?"

"No," Harrison said, confusion on his face. "Not yet. Can he do that?"

Gethen didn't answer, making a note on his page and frowning. "Is there anything?" he asked, though the question wasn't directed at Harrison. Next to him, Devlyn reached over and placed a tattooed hand on his head.

The static surged in his mind and Harrison stumbled in the chair. It felt like the fuzz in his brain was seeping into his every thought, conscious or not, and it overtook him. He couldn't feel his face or much of anything else, his vision going momentarily white. He thought he could smell something burning, but his insides were cold and numb. He didn't know how long he was like that, but it felt like an eternity.

And then it was over as quickly as it began. Devlyn pulled her hand back and turned back to Gethen. She shook her head no.

Gethen let out a noise before he made his final note. "That's all," he said. A smile split his face. "Painless. You're free to go."

Gethen sat down and Harrison took his leave gratefully, scrambling out of the chair and back to the door. The static continued to buzz in his mind and wouldn't quite let him go, though at least his body would obey him. He couldn't quite feel his fingers or toes and his head was starting to pound now that he was away from there. Harrison made his way back down toward the testing labs and a bed so he could try to just sleep this off.

CHAPTER SEVEN

HOMEWORK, HE KNEW, was just a way to keep them busy so that they would stay out of the way. Harrison had been put in Max's old room right next to the closed wing, which suited him fine for now. His room had a larger desk that he and Ally dragged it next to the bed so they could both work off of it.

At least, they both started on the desk. Harrison was soon sitting on the bed with his back against the wall, computer in his lap while Ally sat across from him on the desk with her notes and books taking over. Her fingers flew across the keyboard as her attention switched from books to the screen to her notes.

He glowered down at the screen in front of him, running a hand over his smooth chin. This was the last thing he wanted to be doing while he was essentially detained, but Emma had gone through the trouble of getting their stuff from the other side of the country. He should probably still at least do something normal. He did still have homework, even if he couldn't actually attend his classes this week.

He hoped this wouldn't take more than a week. How long could it possibly take to find Willow and rescue Max?

"You know you're going to pass," Harrison told Ally. "Even if they don't let us out for a while, H&B is going to make sure we aren't going to fail because we were stuck in here. You don't have to do any of this. *We* don't have to do any of this."

Ally let out sharp hum that meant that he was supposed to shut up and go back to what he was doing. Harrison had no interest in deconstructing *Nadja* right now. He didn't even want to read it, not while he was in here. He wanted to know what was going on. Kenzie hadn't been back since that day and Doctor Gethen had taken up permanent residence inside his office. Harrison had seen Devlyn once more following him, but she was still dead eyed and didn't even make eye contact. He was starting to consider a nice walk back to the hospital where he might be able to talk to Emma.

"Ally," Harrison repeated, trying to get her to look up from her screen. "This is stupid. You will pass."

"I don't want to just *pass*," she insisted. "If I don't get how this works, I'm going to be so behind next semester."

"You'll figure it out," he told her. "There's probably a tutorial for doing... whatever that is."

"Most of the ones online are for chatbot AIs," she told him, her eyes going to the screen and her notes once more. "Talking is one thing. Making a robot respond properly to physical input is harder."

"I thought you didn't get to build robots yet."

"I mean, I don't actually get to do that part of the code yet." Ally let out a frustrated sigh and finally tore her eyes away from the screen. "I'm missing all the electronics labs right now, but it's really a lot more taking stuff apart and putting it back together right now. Building from scratch is a little ways off."

"I cannot believe you get to do that stuff in first year."

"You should have asked H&B," she told him. "They got me into the accelerated program. I mean, the studying for it was hell and all, but—"

Harrison was grateful for the opening door. Right now, he didn't want to hear about how much H&B was doing for anyone. Ally didn't seem to think that much about how very detained they were, or the fact that she was very likely going to be stopped at the door if she left. At least he could leave whenever he wanted. He really should just go...

"Hey, you guys in here?" Jack peered into the room and spotted them, a backpack on his back. He didn't wait for an invitation before he let himself in and dropped his bag next to the bed. He sat on the edge of it, pulling out a laptop and a textbook, dropping both onto the table and on the corner of Ally's notes.

"When the hell did you get back?" Harrison asked.

He looked much better than the last time Harrison had seen him. He'd mostly cleaned up, though there were bruises running up his arms. He folded one leg under him, Harrison seeing a bloom of red under the bandage and a patchwork of purple and black peeking out from the edges. There didn't appear to be anything wrong with his face, at least. The scars creeping up under his collar and clawing across the right side of his face had been there since Ally had set him on fire. "Move some of your stuff," he told Ally, already pushing some of her papers out of the way. "I have shit to do too."

Ally stayed very still across from him, watching as her papers moved. Harrison waited to see if she would snap at him for touching them, but she said nothing, not even looking away from her computer. Her fingers stayed poised on the keys, but there was no typing, only a gentle tap like she was thinking about what to do next. Her eyes strayed to the corner of the screen, then back to the center of it, not quite looking at Jack as he settled in.

"You know we're going to pass these classes, right?" Harrison said, closing his laptop. "H&B is taking care of it so they can keep us here."

Jack shrugged. "It's not my homework. Mary's going to be pissed if she gets anything less than a B, and H&B didn't really do a great job keeping her GPA up last semester when they made her stay in for a week."

"You're doing *her* homework?"

"I'm better at it. It's boring as hell, though." He opened one of the books, but he glanced up at Ally as she continued to stay frozen across from them. "What's her deal?" he asked.

"Ally thinks you're still pissed about setting you on fire."

Behind the computer, Ally straightened up. Her eyes were wide and she stared directly at Harrison, jaw clenched and looking betrayed.

Next to him, Jack shrugged again and flipped through the book. "I mean, it sucked, but it happened," he said, repeating the words as he had so many times before. To Harrison, it sounded rehearsed now. "Luke messed with your head and used you as a match. And I regrew most of the skin. Time to move on, right?"

"When did you get here?" Harrison asked, ignoring how Ally continued to look at him. It was a good enough distraction from having to catch up on readings and essays. "I thought they were going to leave you in the hospital for a while."

"It's just a concussion. I won't even notice another one."

"You ever thought about a helmet?"

"For what? Life?"

"Might be an idea."

"You sound like Mary."

"*What happened?*" Ally snapped.

Jack let out a surprised laugh and looked back at her, raising his arms in triumph. "She speaks!"

Ally flushed, but her eyes continued to bore into Jack. She didn't blink, forcing herself not to look away, though her eyes were doing their best not to stare at the scar she had given him. "You can't just walk in here like this and *not* tell us what happened. You were in the hospital! There was blood all over the place!"

"Which time?" Jack grinned at her, trying to sound innocent and utterly failing as the laugh crept back into his words. "Be specific, Allison, or I won't be able to figure out what you're talking about."

Ally only got redder, but she did not look away. Her backbone, it seemed, had returned and it was starting to go back to the way it had been before. Harrison wasn't sure if that was actually a good thing, but at least they were talking to one another.

Jack sighed and relaxed back on the bed, leaning on his hands and looking up at the ceiling. "Fine," he said. "I'm not entirely sure what happened. One minute I'm making dinner, the next the lock for the door is flying across the room and Willow's walking in. She does that... *thing* —" He made a motion with his hand like he was crushing a can before tossing it to the side "— and just chucks me into the bedroom. And then she follows me in and Mary decides the best thing to do is to chuck me out of the way and drop a bed on me. Don't know about the blood, though. No one mentioned that part."

It took Harrison a moment to figure out what about the story was bothering him. "Wait, so *Mary* was the—"

Jack fixed him with a flat stare and Harrison fell silent. He could see the judgement on his face. It was like he expected Harrison to know better. And really, he did.

"No," Harrison conceded. "No, I see it." He could absolutely see Mary doing something that reckless to keep Jack from trying to jump in.

"Both of you have terrible choice in partners," Ally noted.

"Why, did Max beat the shit out of you too?" Jack asked, a broad smile across his face once again. "What did you do to piss him off that much?"

"No. He broke up with me."

"*Again?*" Jack asked. The laugh was back. "I swear, H&B have been trying to break you guys up since they got here."

"I think he—"

Jack smacked him hard in the arm. "He *never* means it," Jack told him. "You really gotta stop visiting while H&B has their test time with him. It screws up Mary really bad too when they have her in for a while. Always takes her at least a couple days to get all the way back to normal."

"It might not be a bad idea if you guys take a break for a while anyway," Ally said. "Save me from coming home early to snap you out of a damn coma."

"Oh, so you're still a bitch," Jack noted. "Good to know nothing's changed."

Ally got to her feet, leaning across the table. Her face was bright red. "Has Mary sent you across the country to starve yourself for days because she's getting a little stressed?" she demanded. "*Multiple times?*"

"I don't know," Jack said. "Have you stopped setting people you don't like on fire?"

It was not a good thing that they were back to normal, Harrison decided, and he wanted no part in this. They could go on like this for a while and they wouldn't even notice he left. Times like this, he could catch a movie, but his mind was turning far too much for him to remember where the theater was. Not that it mattered. There were plenty of places around here to get away from the two of them.

Harrison appeared on the other side of the locked doors in the closed off wing a moment later. He knew he was on the other side of those doors, except this was... not where he was trying to go. It was another empty room much like his own, but it looked like no one had ever inhabited it. There weren't even sheets on the bed, the only light coming from the window and a layer of dust over just about everything. He thought little of it, letting himself out and into the dark, quiet corridor.

That was strange, but he didn't let himself think anything of it.

Their words turned over in his mind. Something about them bothered him. He knew somewhere that Jack was right. It was definitely a pattern and Max had never meant to do this. And it did take him a while before he would reach out to make things up to him. That wasn't unusual and it would have probably happened again if Willow hadn't gotten involved.

But Ally did have a point. Max kept sending him away every time and, though he couldn't quite remember it, he didn't doubt that this had happened before. If they couldn't learn to work things out together, then that was a problem, especially if he couldn't even remember it. And eventually they were going to have to deal with this. But it would have to wait until after they got him back.

If Jack was right.

He hoped Jack was right.

At the very least, if he was going to be in here for a while, he should let his family know he was all right. His parents were out of town, but his sister might want to know he wasn't going to be around for a lot longer than originally intended. He slipped his hand into his back pocket, finding it empty.

He'd left it back in there with Ally and Jack. Damn.

Harrison let out a slow breath. He could just pop in and pop out. Maybe they wouldn't even notice him.

A moment later, he was fairly certain he was not in Max's dorm room. At least, he was pretty sure this wasn't it. Blinking,

Harrison looked around, seeing that there was a ruined bed that had been tossed into a wall, and very little else. The wall still had remnants of something on it. Glass lay scattered in shards across the floor, though there was little else here except for the feeling that he needed to get out of there. Now.

Except that he couldn't seem to figure out what was wrong about this place. There was something very strange about this room, something that didn't make sense, but also something comforting and familiar. He knew he didn't want to be in here, but he wasn't sure why. It was probably not the room he was trying to get to, but he couldn't quite remember where he was going anymore. There was something very nice about this room. He could stay a little longer.

And yet, his heart pounded in his chest with the need to go anywhere but here.

His legs felt weak as he walked to the door. There was something low, something lingering in his head that made it hard to concentrate on anything. His sense of where exactly he was had vanished and he couldn't just teleport away. But there was a door, and the doors to these rooms were always unlocked.

Except this one.

Curious, Harrison looked at the door like it had offended him. It should have opened. He tried the knob again, turning it this way and that, but it wouldn't budge. He threw his shoulder into the door, but it stuck, not moving an inch. Around him, the world tilted and his head spun, letting that strange feeling of comfort and unease overpower him.

He finally figured out what was so nice about this room. Creeping quietly into his brain and building inside of it, now the static was loud enough to make out. It sounded like Max, but also very unlike him. "It's gonna be okay," he muttered as he sank down to the ground. "We're going to be okay."

CHAPTER EIGHT

HARRISON WANTED OUT of there. He wasn't sure how long he was sitting on the floor against the door, but it didn't really matter. He couldn't do much while he was down here anyway. Even though he could still feel his feet, he wasn't entirely certain where they were. He could feel the floor against his hands, but couldn't quite remember how to use them to pick himself up. He knew he should be worried about that, but it was difficult to make himself care about anything.

The door trembled against his face, and the ground followed suit. Harrison pushed himself away from it and held onto the shaking ground, watching as the door shook and the frame cracked. The door swung inward and knocked Harrison back, a figure standing in the doorway and looking frantically around, yelling something. He was pretty sure he was calling for Mary.

Harrison blinked up at him. Jack. That was Jack. And he was standing. That was the direction that up was. He could do that.

"Harrison?" he asked, his eyes narrowing as he looked around the room. He bent down and offered him a hand up. "The fuck are you doing in here?"

"I missed," he said. Harrison took his hand and Jack yanked him to his feet hard enough that he stumbled into him. Jack pulled him out of the room and looped his arm around his shoulders, hauling him back to the doors out of this wing. "I was trying to get back and I missed."

"I thought you couldn't *miss*."

"I guess I can."

Jack threw the doors open and dragged him through. Harrison was fairly certain that they were supposed to be locked, but he was also pretty sure they were also still fully on their hinges the last time he saw them. They were decidedly not any longer.

"You're wrecking the place," Harrison noted. His head was already starting to clear from the fuzz that had overwhelmed it. He could walk on his own and Jack let him, Harrison leading them away from Max's room and further down the hall to anyone else's. He ran his hands over his face, pressing his fingers into his eyes. He was going to have a headache later.

"It sounded like Mary," Jack said. "But that would have been too easy."

"Yeah. Sounds like Max in there too."

"So when are we getting out of here to find them?"

Harrison looked at him, trying to figure out if he was serious.

"What?" Jack demanded. "You weren't thinking about leaving me out of this, were you? I'm going with you. We're going to get them back. They can't keep us from leaving."

"We have to let H&B do this," Harrison said. "We don't stand a chance against Willow."

Betrayal flickered over Jack's face for only a moment before he glanced up, noting one of the cameras. "It's fine," he insisted. "No one's actually watching those. And even if they were, the hell are they going to do about it?"

Harrison shook his head. He could hear sounds coming from one of the doors and steered them toward it. "We don't even know where they went," Harrison told him. "And it's *Willow*. Did you see what she did to Adam? What are we even going to do?"

"Get in, grab them, get out. It's not that complicated. You can do it."

"So why am I bringing you?" he asked, pushing the door open. It was Ted's room, and one that looked much more lived in. They were free to stay if they wanted, and Ted had decided to make it a second home. There were books and comics in here, along with a small collection of DVDs for when the internet wouldn't quite work properly. He'd pulled a few extra chairs in from somewhere else in the building and arranged the place more like a living room than a temporary place to sleep between tests. Ally had already decided to stop in, sitting on the floor with a book while Ted put his own down next to him.

"Everyone's just going to let themselves in here, aren't they?" Ted asked, though he did nothing to stop them.

"To make sure you don't run before you grab them," Jack said. He looked around and nodded to Ted. "Hey, thanks for getting that bed off me."

"No problem," Ted said, looking concerned. Ally was pretending not to pay attention, but she had stopped moving entirely and Harrison knew she was listening. "Grab who?"

"Max and Mary," Jack said. "Should be easy. We track them down, Harrison pops us in and out before Willow knows we're there, and we're good. Just have to make sure he doesn't lose his nerve half way through."

"You mean come to my senses?"

"We probably won't even see her."

"Do you know where they are?" Ally asked, genuinely hopeful. "Did they find something?"

Jack let out a derisive laugh. "No," he said. "But really, how hard could it be to find them? They're with Willow, so you'll be able to hear them a block away."

"So your plan is to wander around and hope you find them," Ally said, moving so she could sit against the bed. "Just leave it to H&B, Jack. They're going to be a lot better than us at finding them."

"I mean, they didn't look for Jack in his own place," Ted pointed out. He kept looking back and forth between Ally and Jack, not sure what was happening.

"They're just keeping us here and hoping Willow finds us and you know it," Jack said. "We can't just sit here and do nothing."

"I thought *you* were going to do something."

"I thought you were going to stop being a *bitch*, but it looks like we can't all get what we want."

"*Whoa*," Ted said, getting to his feet. "What the hell, guys?"

"Don't," Harrison warned him as he looked through the comics. He could at least get something to flip through until they were done. "They'll get tired eventually."

"Okay, *fine*," Ally snapped back, not paying any attention to Ted. "So you wander around until you think you hear them. Where are you going to start? Because it's been a few days. And if Harrison can get across the country in one, then Willow could have taken them anywhere by now."

"We can find them!" Jack yelled back. "Where the hell would she go?"

"That's what I'm asking!"

Jack opened his mouth to reply, then closed it again. His jaw clenched tight as they glared at one another, fuming.

"Told you," Harrison said, dropping down next to Ted on the bed. He opened the book and started looking through it. "You know where Jaime is? Seems like she should be stuck in here dealing with this too."

"God, you guys must have been so happy when you replaced him with me," Ted said quietly. It wasn't quietly enough, but neither of them was paying any attention.

"I mean," Harrison said, trying to figure out the words. "There were circumstances."

"I haven't seen Jaime since the hospital," Ted said, clearly not wanting to touch those circumstances right now. "Apparently Adam's doing better, though. They're supposed to be—"

The knock at the door silenced them. "Finally, someone with manners," Ted muttered. He got to his feet and opened it, Kenzie standing nervously on the other side.

"Hey," she said. "Hope I'm not interrupting anything. Doctor Gethen wanted Harrison and Jack for something."

———◆———

HARRISON KNEW BETTER than to ask what was happening, but that did nothing to stop Jack. Kenzie had no answers for them, though she did try. It was just more testing, as far as she knew, and Gethen wanted to get more involved in the process. He had ideas that he felt they were not being implemented and it was time they did it properly.

Jack didn't look impressed by that, and Harrison knew why. That didn't sound at all like he was focusing on trying to find Willow or get Max and Mary back. If that wasn't what he was doing, then what was the point of him being here?

They went into a small lab, smaller than the ones Harrison was used to. Kenzie left them at the door and Devlyn was there to meet them.

"Hey," Harrison signed.

She didn't respond, leading them to the back of the room and directing them into the two chairs sitting there. A low hum echoed in his mind.

Jack leaned over, arms crossed and leaning back in his chair. "You know her?"

Harrison nodded, watching her. "She's from the Orlando office." She still looked dead eyed and lifeless. Harrison was starting to wonder if the one time he had seen her before was the anomaly or if it was this one. "She used to be more chatty."

The door opened again and Doctor Gethen came in, papers in hand. He adjusted his glasses and a pleasant smile spread across his face. Immediately, Harrison didn't trust it. "We're going to be trying something new with you two today," he said. "See if your respective partners have rubbed off on you so far."

"How the hell would they have done that?" Jack asked.

"I'll be cracking a few things open in your heads to see just what we can encourage," he continued. The smile that crept over his face only just held back his irritation. "Don't worry. Harrish and Barrister require a light touch. But if you'll be in here for a little while anyway..."

"Shouldn't you be trying to find Willow?" Jack demanded. "If you're going to keep us locked up in here, then—"

Gethen wasn't impressed. He made a gesture and said something to Devlyn.

Harrison's vision went white. His mind and body were nothing but that buzzing feeling. There was no sound, no smell, no light, only the static penetrating every part of his being. He didn't know if he was still sitting, not even able to feel the chair underneath him. Whatever happened next, Harrison didn't know.

CHAPTER NINE

THUMP. THUMP. THUMP.

Whatever that was, it was growing louder and the darkness was getting less dark. Things came back in pieces. The hard, rough ground underneath him. The strange cold in the air. The knowledge that it should be warmer. His fingers still tingled as if they had fallen asleep. There was a static laying heavy on his mind that was not his own.

Willow.

Her face flashed through his mind, the last thing he'd seen before he lost consciousness. His body went rigid, mind suddenly very alert and trying to piece together what was going on. He was drawing a blank and his body didn't feel the need to wake up any faster to try and help him figure things out.

Max convinced his eyes to crack open so he could slowly take in the room around him. It was small and dark, though not for lack of trying. There were windows along the top of the wall to let the light in, but up too high for him to reach. It was night outside, it seemed, and the only illumination was very artificial and colourful. He could hear traffic.

He'd been in this room for a while. He'd woken up in here before.

The banging that woke him up came from the door, a girl he knew well running into it over and over again with her shoulder. He knew Mary's bushy hair and stocky build as it flew into the door, as well as the steady stream of cursing that followed her bouncing back off of it.

And there was no one else. Willow wasn't there.

"Mary?" Max asked, opening his eyes wider and looking around before he raised his voice any more. His body grew more cooperative the longer he was awake. He could feel his legs now. "Where are we?" He tried to push himself up, but the wave of dizziness hit as soon as he got his hands underneath him. He sagged against his arms, letting his head drop down to the cool concrete with a groan.

"Max!" Mary was at his side in an instant, hand on his back and static buzzing heavy in his head. "I thought she actually killed you that time."

"You're buzzing real loud."

"Oh."

Max understood, but he appreciated that Mary tried to pull it back. It was something that just happened with them, especially when they were stressed, but his head already felt so muddled that it wasn't helping. He closed his eyes, trying to catch the breath he didn't realize he'd lost and let Mary help him sit.

"Sorry," he said, taking another look around. Behind him, there was a mattress on the ground that looked like it had been slept in, as well as a few bags of 7/11 filled with garbage and smelled of food that should have been thrown out. He could see no way out except for the door. "Where are we?"

Mary shook her head, frowning and looking like she still had a lot more swearing left in her. "Still no idea," she said. "And I don't know how you got here. Willow just showed up in my place and just grabbed me and dropped me here. And she's not here right now, so try to relax. If you give it a few minutes, it will start coming back to you again. How are—"

"Where's Jack?" Max was starting to feel better already and folded his legs in front of him. His thoughts were getting clearer, but coming back out of order. He wanted to know where Willow was and where she had gone. He knew he had been here for a while with Willow before Mary showed up. He knew he had seen a massacre somewhere. And he knew he had asked Mary this question before.

"I kept him out of the way," Mary said, though her look was uncertain. Her shoulders came up to her ears and she wouldn't look him in the face. She had answered this way before. "He was going to try to be a hero if I didn't. And she was only coming after me."

"Sounds like him," he said. Mary didn't like that question. For as much as she tried, the buzzing wasn't getting any quieter while she was thinking about it. "Is Willow still leaving you alone?"

Mary hesitated a moment before she nodded. He could hear her buzzing still, low and insistent, though Max imagined he wasn't much better right now. He imagined that if they were left to it, they could probably knock someone out with how loud they both were. He wondered if it might be enough to make Willow leave him alone.

He knew it wasn't. They had already tried it.

For now, he tried to put the jumble of thoughts in his head in an order, to place the sequence back in place. There was an order to them, and things that he could only speculate about. He was missing parts, but as soon as he looked at the blanks in his memory they filled again. He needed to just figure out what he knew and put it together.

"It's fine," she said. "Tell me what you know." Max blinked at her for a moment, wondering if he had said something. He knew he hadn't. He was thinking everything very loudly, and Mary could hear it. Much in the same way he could hear that Mary was doing her best to be patient and wanted him to hurry up so they could come up with a new plan.

"I don't know what happened," he told her. "I was at work and people were screaming outside. And there was..." Max faltered, remembering the red everywhere. A knot formed in the pit of his stomach, remembering the metallic taste in the air, and the low gurgling moan of someone he didn't see, barely audible over the crowd keeping their distance. One he knew, but his mind refused to place. There was no need to tell her any of that. "And then there was Willow. And then I'm here. And… and then she brought you here. But she wants something from me."

"That's about right," Mary told him. "I don't know why you went to work. You *just* got out of testing, Max. Not that it would have probably stopped her. She was supposed to be a vegetable."

"And on the other side of the country. We need to get out of here."

"Yes we do."

"So the door's locked?" Max asked, looking around for another way out. His eyes drifted upward to the faint light streaming in above them. "You think we could reach the windows?"

"Maybe if you could stand up, I could lift you. It doesn't look like there's a latch or anything up there, though."

Max frowned, but tried to push himself up anyway. Mary was at his side to help him up a moment later, though Max could already feel a wave of nausea wash over him. It wasn't dizziness that followed as he managed to stand on his own feet, but static that filled his head. Static that was most definitely not from Mary. Gripping her shoulder to steady himself, he clenched his eyes shut and tried to push it away.

Not now. Please not now.

"You okay?" Mary asked.

"Fine."

"Let me rephrase. You look like shit. Sit down."

"I'm *fine*, Mary." He still let her lower him back down to the ground, putting him against the wall. He brought his knees up enough to rest his arms on them and let his head drop. His eyes closed tight and he tried to push the static back and away. He'd already dealt with this enough the past few days and he didn't need any more of it. It had already made him...

"I've been meaning to ask," Mary said after a moment. "What happened with Harrison?"

Max glanced over, but she wasn't even looking at him. She knew he was starting to get in his own head, and Harrison was the easiest way to pull him back out, but that wasn't the only thing she had to worry about right now. She only had eyes for the wall, running her hand over it. He let out a sigh. Well, if he wasn't going to be any help getting up there, then she might as well try climbing the thing. It was better than just sitting here and waiting for something to happen.

"I tried calling him before," she continued. "His phone was off. And I heard he didn't finish his round of testing."

"We broke up." As much as Max didn't want to think about it, the thought of what happened seemed to be enough to help push back some of that static in his head. He let his head fall back against the wall, letting out a deep sigh. Mary already knew this, but he would tell her again. "I told him to go home. And he did."

"You made him go back, though. He didn't want to do it. You *made* him."

"I didn't mean to, I just..." He didn't know how to explain it, or if he wanted to. That static lingered in the back of his head. There was something that happened when he went in for testing. It felt like there was something else in there trying to get out and it was terrifying. Even thinking about it made him feel it creeping back into his consciousness.

"We'll figure out how to make you stop doing that," Mary said. She could tell he was slipping away again. "For right now, just try to keep calm, okay? We'll make sure you can call Harrison when we get out of this and explain what happened."

"Sorry," he said. He was buzzing and he knew it. He needed to at least try and focus. Outside, he could hear a very distinctive bell, but he couldn't quite place where he knew it from. "Where is here? Did you figure out anything else?"

Any distraction from whatever was happening in his head right now was welcome. They'd gotten off topic. They were trapped in a random room with a locked door blocking their way out. Willow would probably be back soon enough and they only had a matter of time to get out of there. Max being an idiot and breaking up with his boyfriend by accident was the least of their worries. Even if Harrison could probably get them out of here.

"Hell if I know." Mary was back at the wall and he could feel it rattling behind him. Mary didn't sound or look particularly pleased with whatever was happening, Max looking back to the door as she muttered, "I swear that thing sounds like I should know it. Where's Ted when you need him? He can usually figure this stuff out..."

Max's breath caught as a thought came to him, overpowering and terrifying. She was on her way.

Willow.

Mary stopped, but Max didn't know if it was because she had heard him or if she had felt it too. Their eyes both went to the door. It was still closed but the space in front of it was now occupied. The young woman who had helped smuggle him across the border to throw into an incinerator stood there now and they had run out of time.

Willow looked thinner than before, cheeks sunken in and complexion even paler than before. Where she had found herself another black dress that looked like it came out of a Tim Burton movie, he had no idea, but it was far less distracting than the mildly confused expression on her face. Her red eyes looked between the pair of them and she tossed a plastic bag on the mattress.

Mary was already advancing on her before Max could try to stop her. "You can't just keep us locked away in here!" she yelled at her. Max saw Willow twitch on her feet, a frown growing on her pale face and her red eyes narrowing as Mary got closer. "If you don't let us—"

Mary took flight across the room, her last word leaving her along with the rest of the air in her lungs as soon as her feet left the ground. She slammed hard into the wall, feet kicking wildly as the rest of her struggled to move. Her face went red, muscles in her jaw tightening as if she were trying to say something. All that came out were a series of muffled screams.

Max pressed himself against the wall, using it to keep himself upright and looking around for a place to run. Anywhere. His heart hammered hard in his chest as he looked from corner to corner for anything besides that mattress that might offer him something. There was nothing in the room to hide behind, and Willow was already staring at him.

And then Willow was in front of him, her hands on his shoulders. It was now that Max realized he was shaking, but he tried to stay still. Those red eyes studied him carefully. She ignored Mary's struggles and attempts to scream. Willow's lips didn't move, but he could hear her voice in his ears as clearly as if she were actually talking. *Are you out yet?*

Max wasn't even sure he was breathing anymore. She was so close, staring so carefully at him. He had nowhere to go, and even if he wanted to run, his body wouldn't move. His mind was paralyzed with the need to do something, but no idea what he could do. Lingering in the back of his mind, the foreign static was growing stronger.

Not yet. Willow smiled, pulling her face back just a little. *Time for you to let him go now.*

At first, there was nothing but that determined grin on Willow's face. Maybe something had stopped her. Maybe Harrison had shown up with the cavalry and they were standing right behind him.

He hoped Harrison wasn't here right now.

Then, lancing through his arms into his body, there was nothing but pain as his every muscle contracted on its own. Everything felt like it had caught on fire and sparks danced over his eyes, the air leaving his lungs with a howl that ripped through his throat. Unconsciousness was a welcome relief.

CHAPTER TEN

HARRISON WOKE WITH a start, heart pounding hard in his chest. Images swirled through his mind and Max's name was on his lips. He'd seen Max and he was not doing well. He had to get him out of there now. They needed to go before anything else happened. Out of that barren room. He could get them. Both of them. They needed to get out of there before...

He tried to catch his breath and took in where he was right now. The room was dark, but it was larger and didn't have the same light streaming in above him. His body was numb, pins and needles starting to form across his skin that threatened to become much more painful if he tried to move. He was still in H&B, nowhere near wherever Max had been. Max was still missing, and he wasn't in any position to do anything about it. It was only a dream.

It had felt almost real at times and distant at others, though he struggled to piece together the details. At times he could almost tell where it was, the location *feeling* familiar, but it was never quite enough to figure out where. If he just had a reference, then maybe he could, but the room had told him nothing.

And it was, he reminded himself as he took in a very deep breath, only a dream. After what Doctor Gethen had put him and Jack through, it was no wonder he was having nightmares.

He wasn't sure what the plan had been, but Harrison had experienced nothing but blinding static for as long as he was in that room. He was supposed to do something about it, to make it stop or make some of his own to make it go away, maybe to figure out what parts of his head were his own and which were Devlyn creeping into his mind. He didn't know when it had stopped or when he'd gotten to bed, but he was already dreading having to do it again. And Doctor Gethen would ask them both to do it again.

Still, the dream wouldn't leave him. Even as the feeling started to come back into his limbs and he managed to sit up, he felt like he should do something about it. He was, however, at a loss for where the dream took place. He could go check it out, if only to tell himself that it was definitely all in his head, but he had no idea where it was.

And there was the problem of if it *was* all real. If Willow...

His door banged open and he jumped back in the small metal bed. Jack appeared in his doorway. He slammed on the light and looked wildly around until he found Harrison sitting in his bed. He looked like he had shot right out of bed to come here, breathing heavy with just about everything about him disheveled. He wore only a shirt that was askew and a pair of boxers as he fixed Harrison with wild green eyes. "We need to go. I know where they are."

Harrison let out a deep breath, shaking his head as he waited for his heart to calm down. "At least put on some pants," he said, massaging his hands. The feeling wasn't quite back in them yet. Or in his legs. "Nearly gave me a damn heart attack."

"I know where Mary and Max are! We have to go now."

That sounded... wrong. Harrison peered at him, trying to determine if he was still dreaming. The tingling in his hands and feet was very insistent that he wasn't. Even through the bleariness of the hour, Harrison knew there was no way Jack had suddenly developed the ability to locate Max, but stranger things had happened. Like spontaneously developing the ability to teleport before getting abducted by crazy people. "*Where?*" he asked, already feeling stupid for going along with this. "Why do you even know?"

"They're on the MAX. Stop asking stupid shit, let's go!" Jack moved across the room to Harrison's side. Harrison shifted away, but not fast enough as Jack tried to grab his arm. He felt a tingle run through his shoulder. A bright blue flash of light passed through Harrison into Jack's hand. Jack snapped back his hand, looking accusingly at Harrison. "The hell was that?" he demanded.

Harrison heard someone knocking on a door. Ted peered into the room a moment later, looking between the pair of them and shaking his head. He stayed quiet for the moment.

"I think that's called static electricity," Harrison told Jack, nodding at the door. "You're being too damn loud, by the way."

"And Mary being on Max doesn't sound right," Ted said. He leaned back out of the doorway again, knocking hard on the next door. "Come on, if it woke me up then it woke you up too!"

Harrison heard Ally's muffled protests coming from the next room as Ted let himself in and dropped down onto the bed. Ally appeared in the door a moment later, looking like she was ready to set someone on fire as she glared from Jack to Ted. "This had better be worth it."

"I think Jack found Max and Mary," Ted offered. He looked back to Harrison, eyes narrowing down at where he was massaging his hands. "What happened to you?"

"Slept funny."

"I *did* find them! They're right on the MAX."

"Oh, like the *train*," Ted clarified.

"They're hanging out on a train," Ally repeated, unimpressed. "I'm going back to bed."

"Not *on* the train, on the line. I could hear it going past. They're in some basement somewhere on the line. Willow's got them and she's... I don't know what she's doing, but..."

Harrison frowned at that. It sounded familiar, like something that was fading away faster than the tingling in his fingers. "With the windows along the top of the wall?" Harrison asked, not looking up from his fingers. "And Mary couldn't get the door open."

"And Max looked like he wasn't doing so hot."

He could feel the eyes on him, but Harrison didn't look up. His eyes stayed on his fingers and trying to massage the feeling back into them, his mind turning over what he saw over and over. Part of him wanted to think it was just the hour, the daylight barely creeping in to signal the start of the day, but he could still remember the sparks that flashed over his vision at the end, and the tingle that was only now starting to fade from his hands and feet.

"So you know I'm right," Jack said. "Come on, we have to go *now*."

If Jack had seen it too, and if it felt so real, then he had to go there to be sure. Part of him hoped that it was really all in their heads, that they had both just happened to have the same dream as a side effect of whatever Doctor Gethen was trying to do. If it was real, Max was suffering and Willow really was back and after something.

"Wait, no," Ally said, her hands dragging over her face. "This is stupid. What's going on?"

"*I saw them,*" Jack insisted. "I could hear the MAX go past. We can find them if we stop sitting around and just go!"

"The MAX goes past a lot, Jack," Ted told him, getting slowly to his feet. Jack was already pacing, his hands moving wildly through the air and gesturing at nothing as if demanding that the universe tell him why no one was listening to him.

Ted, tired though he was, did his best to calm him down. "I mean it sounds like this... this might actually be a lead." Harrison could feel the eyes glance back at him, but he didn't look up. "But you can't just pop into every basement along all three MAX lines to see if they're there. You guys were both a little messed up from testing yesterday."

"Let H&B deal with it."

Harrison looked around the room and saw nothing, though Ally didn't look remotely surprised to hear Jaime's voice in the room. He followed her eye line down, shifting on the bed and looking around Ted to find Jaime sitting on the ground against the metal frame. A faint glow lit her up, Harrison able to see the phone now in her hands for a moment before she put it back down. He knew better than to ask when she had gotten there.

"What the hell are *they* going to do that we can't?" Jack demanded.

"Actually send enough people to find one basement some- where along one of the MAX lines?" Ted offered. "Jaime, they've been looking, right?"

"Top priority is finding Willow," Jaime confirmed. "Second is keeping us all in one place until she comes after the rest of us."

"Why would she even want the rest of us?"

"Why did she go after Max and Mary?" Ally asked. "It's not like any of this is making any sense. Come on, we might as well just get back to sleep and deal with it in the morning."

"She *isn't* after the rest of us!" Jack insisted, stepping closer to Ally. "If she was, she wouldn't have left me—"

"Woah!" Ted said, getting between them before Jack got too close to her. "Look. This whole thing is messed up, but we got a lead. It's progress, right? We just need to tell H&B and they'll send people after her. And if they smoke her out, she'll probably be heading for the rest us, so we need to stay put for a bit."

Jack let out a heavy breath, irritation filling his shoulders and his arms crossed. The glare he shot went through Ted and passed around the room, Harrison feeling the eyes settle on him like he was meant to back him up here.

But Harrison was stuck in his own head, now grasping for those last details. He pushed back the guilt of trying to pass it off as a dream, of hoping that it was only that so that he wouldn't have to do anything, and replaced it with searching the memory for something he could use. He could feel generally where it was, and Jack was convinced it was on the MAX line. He could almost place where it was. Almost.

"They've already got a team on it," Jaime told them. "And someone on the way here to talk to you guys to get more information. Finding Willow is top priority."

"What about the people she's kidnapped?" Jack demanded. "They planning to do anything to rescue Mary out of that place?"

"Priority is Willow," Jaime repeated. "By any means necessary. And once they have her, they'll—"

"*Any means?*" Jack roared. "So they might kill her to get to Willow, that's what you're telling me?"

It was much too loud to put anything together in here. He was so close to figuring it out, if only he had a bit of quiet to put it together. "I'm going for a walk." His voice was quiet as he spoke, but he didn't care if anyone heard him. He was gone a moment later.

CHAPTER ELEVEN

THE AIR IN the Hayes building never felt stale until he got outside. Everything felt a lot more clear out here, even at the early hour. The dew already started to cling to the grass and birds flitted back and forth over his head. The cool early morning of spring helped clear his head, and it brought to light a few very specific things.

First was that he had no shoes. The second was that he had no pants. He could probably use a shirt too.

He tried to get to Max's at his house room, but appeared instead beneath the tree in his front yard. As infuriating as it was to have missed, he figured standing outside of his boyfriend's place in only his boxers was probably something he should deal with first.

With a little more focus, his second attempt got him where he needed to be. He appeared in Max's room, hit now by the smell of him. Harrison let out a deep breath, shaking his head and running a hand through his hair. It felt strange to be here without Max around, almost like he was spying on him. He wondered if he should have tried the front door, to at least let his parents know that he was here to get some clothes, but he didn't want to face them without being able to tell them where their son was. And he wasn't sure he wanted them to see him in this state of undress.

He turned on the light and looked around. The room was mostly unchanged from the last time he was here. There was dirty laundry on the floor now, and his work bag was gone, but otherwise it was just like the last time. It was probably because Max hadn't been here in a while. He was gone, off dealing with whatever it was Willow was doing to him, while Harrison was breaking in.

Pants. He needed to find pants. His duffel bag was still in the corner, half unpacked and open. Untouched. He grabbed pants and a shirt and threw them on, trying not to let his gaze drift to the rest of the room. He didn't want to get distracted or be in here long enough to wake up Max's parents.

He went for the light to leave when he saw a movement out the window. Harrison froze and looked, ready to run for it. In the house next door, Tara had thrown open a window and was half hanging out of it, waving her arms and trying to make the flashlight of her phone shine in Harrison's face.

Wide eyed and alarmed, he went across to the window. "What are you doing?" he signed furiously. She was definitely going to draw attention, or possibly wake up Max's parents with the light shining so erratically over the side of the house. "Stop!"

Tara didn't understand sign language, he remembered as she started waving him over. She looked relieved that he had seen her. Even if she did understand what he was saying, Harrison doubted that she would have stopped. At least she put her phone away.

She also knew about what he could do. Harrison went back to turn off the light before going back to the window. He gestured for her to step back and waited until she disappeared into her house. He locked eyes with the windowsill and focused, appearing seated on it a moment later.

Whatever he was expecting, Tara's bedroom certainly wasn't it. He'd never been to Tara's house, but somehow he didn't think that her room would face Max's. She ushered him the rest of the way in, closing the window behind him and looking around at the street outside before she closed the curtains.

"Are you supposed to just do this out in public like that?" she asked.

"No." He let his gaze wander and saw Jaime's card on the table next to her bed along with three other identical ones, all of them with the corners frayed like she had been playing with them. He wondered how long H&B had had their sights on her.

"I thought I was bluffing," Tara mumbled. She wouldn't look at him.

Harrison studied her for a moment. He was supposed to be doing other things. He should be trying to find Max. He didn't need to be here right now. "What do you want, Tara? It's the middle of the night."

She hesitated, wrapping her arms around herself. Her eyes went from the window and back to Harrison, trying to put together the words. "Is this like last time?" she asked. "I don't even *know* what happened last time, but Jer was so freaked out and now *I'm* getting freaked out."

Tara's boyfriend, Jeremy, was close to Max, though Harrison thought he took a little too much enjoyment in the attention Max's disappearance had earned him the last time. Max wasn't bothered that his friend was so keen to give interviews about how he'd been listening as Max had gone missing, though this wasn't the time to bring that up.

"It's not like last time," Harrison said. He didn't move from his spot against the wall, staring off into a corner of her room where clothes had been piled onto a chair. This was *very* different from last time. For one thing, Harrison wasn't there. For another, Max was doing much worse than before. But Tara didn't need to know any of that. "H&B are going to find him, though. They'll get him back." He didn't know if he was saying that for himself or for her benefit at this point.

"Do they even know where he is?" He could feel her eyes on him, but he didn't look up. "Do they really know what they're doing?"

"It's going to be okay, Tara," he said. He didn't have time for this. "Look, it's late. You should—"

"Harrison, look at me," she said. "What's going on? What aren't you telling me?"

Harrison's eyes came up, meeting Tara's desperate expression. "Willow came back," he told her. He didn't see the harm in telling her a few things. "We don't know why she's even here or how she's moving around even, and no one's telling us anything. They just rounded us up and they're trying to keep us out of the way and, I don't know. They said it's so that we can lure out Willow, but I don't think she wants the rest of us. Jaime probably knows more than me, but no one's actually told us anything."

"But they know how to find him?"

Harrison shook his head, letting out a breath. He could feel his heart rate rising just thinking about it. The words fell out of him and he couldn't stop them. "I don't know if they do," he said. "I mean, the only lead I know of is this dream Jack and I had and they haven't even— I left before they sent anyone to ask us about it. They still have Jack, though, so they'll get that soon enough."

"Dream." She didn't seem to believe it, but took a breath. "I mean, not the weirdest thing that's happened. You dreamed where he was?"

"Sort of?" He started massaging his hands again, the tingle of a memory coming back stronger now that he was talking about it. "I dreamed about Max, and I could kind of tell where he was. Jack knew that sound was the MAX. I didn't recognize it, but if it was..."

Something else in Harrison pulled him back from continuing. There was a desire, a need to keep going, but something about this felt off. He pressed the heel of his hand into his eye and his fingers toyed with the loose hair hanging in his face. He hadn't slept nearly enough in the last couple days, but he knew that something strange was happening right now.

"But do you know where he is?" Tara pressed. "Like if you really think about it, can you figure out where he is? Like, focus really hard and you'll find it, right?"

He cycled back to his dream and let one hand press into his fingers so hard that they started to go numb again. The room wasn't a place that he'd ever seen before, but when things were clear he could almost *feel* where it was. The MAX, he hadn't really paid attention to it before, but now that Jack had mentioned it he could hear something about it. He knew which part of the tracks that was. They had been past it before. He couldn't quite place it on a map, but he could feel that location. He could probably go there if he wanted to. Harrison blinked. "I think I can."

"Then it can be over soon, right? You can tell them where he is and they can bring him back."

"I... I don't know where," Harrison told her. "It's not an *address* or anything. I just kind of..."

Something was off here and he couldn't put his finger on what it was. His heart was racing. A chance to get them both back was so close, but there was something wrong with it all. Was he even supposed to be telling her anything? "Why are you so on about this?"

"I'm not *on* about anything. Max is my friend and I'm worried about—"

"No, there's something else to this." Harrison fixed her with a gaze, his clouded mind trying to put something together that would work. "Is this about that video?"

"It just— okay, look. I don't even remember taking that video. But, like, looking at it, I know it happened. I saw all of it. And when I close my eyes, I can see bits of it. But I don't remember *any* of it. Jer was having non-stop nightmares until Max got back last time and— and— well, you know where he is! Why don't you go get him? He's your boyfriend, isn't he?"

"She'll kill me if she catches me!" It came out of nowhere but Harrison realized as soon as he said it that this was where all of his hesitation was stemming from. Even if Max hadn't meant to break up with him, even if he really never wanted to see him again, Harrison was willing to deal with the fallout of that if it meant getting him to safety. He was less willing to see Willow again, especially after seeing the video.

Harrison was shaking as another realization struck him. There was something wrong about this whole thing. He didn't normally lose his cool like this. He wasn't usually prone to yelling in people's houses when their parents were asleep, even as exhausted as he was. There was something else he wasn't picking up on. Something that he really should remember right now.

"You don't even need to see her, do you?" she insisted. "You can just go in there and get him out before anyone sees!"

"It might all be a dream," he told her. "It could be *nothing*."

"Then just go look! If you're already there, you could at least have a look. Just check and if it's real then you can get in and get out with him before anyone realizes you're there."

"I..." His brow furrowed as he finally figured out what was happening here. His eyes went back to Tara. She looked tired in the low light, the dark circles under her eyes showing just how little sleep she was getting. He could appreciate how worried she might be, but that wasn't what was bothering him right now.

Static. He could hear the static echoing in his head now, and knew that these things were not things he would have normally said to her. He shouldn't have been able to focus enough to even figure out where Max was, and she was getting too much information out of him for her own good.

"You need to not do that," he told her.

"Do what?"

Harrison was gone before she got her answer.

CHAPTER TWELVE

HE REALIZED WHAT he was missing as soon as his feet hit the pavement of downtown Portland. Shoes. He had forgotten to get shoes.

The cool, jagged pavement on his feet helped to bring his mind back to the present, tearing it away from the effect that Tara was having on him. Part of him knew that Tara hadn't meant it, that she probably didn't even know what she was doing. Max didn't realize he was doing it at first either, not until someone had pointed it out to him. Harrison thought he was getting much better at picking it out, but with Tara he hadn't even been expecting it. He didn't know to be careful. And she didn't even know she was doing it.

He'd said too much. He wasn't sure what was too much, but he was sure something in all of that had crossed a line. He'd realize what it was soon enough.

Harrison ran a hand through his hair and let out a deep breath. His feet were cold and uncomfortable against the concrete, but he didn't care. He was frustrated, but there was nothing to do about it. She didn't know any better. And now he knew to be very careful around Tara.

Still, one thing had come of it. He leaned back against the building where Max was being kept. He doubted he would have been able to figure this out on his own. Even knowing where it was, though, he didn't have an address. He hadn't thought to grab his pants when he left, much less his phone. Not that he necessarily needed to wait for anyone. He could always just go in and get out with him before anyone…

No, that was Tara thinking. Harrison knew he couldn't just appear inside. He was no match for Willow if she was there, and there was no telling if she was or not. He'd have to wait until he was certain she was gone. Or he could listen to his own advice and leave it to H&B.

But he had to figure out where this was. At this hour, he couldn't hear the MAX running, but he knew this street. During the day, it went past here, tripping over the tracks and making that strange clack that Max could never seem to pick out. He didn't know which line it was, but it was something to go off of. If he could find a cross street and a number on this building, he could run back with the information and get someone over here as soon as he could convince them he wasn't crazy.

The first step off the wall made him pause, a fist forming around his heart and tightening. He was right here. He could just go in and make sure Max was okay. He was already right here. And more than just checking for the address, he wanted to know if the dream was real. Part of him hoped it wasn't, not after what he had seen at the end.

If it was real, it was clear that Mary couldn't help Max no matter how she tried. Neither of them knew what Willow wanted. She seemed determined to get something out of Max, and he couldn't help but think Max had an idea of what that was. Harrison couldn't help feeling that something very bad was about to happen. Or that it might have already. He wasn't even sure how long ago that was or if it was real. But he was already here. He could check. Just one look...

But Willow.

He took another step forward, and stopped. He couldn't be scared of Willow now. He'd lived with her for long enough and she wasn't a threat then. Yes, she turned out to be terrifying, but she was also a vegetable for the past year, unresponsive and unable to do anything to hurt anyone. She probably wasn't up to her full potential yet. And Harrison was faster than she was when it came to running for it.

Except he'd seen Adam. And he'd seen Mary. And he knew full well what else she was capable of now that the dust had been cleared from his eyes. Even without Luke, she was dangerous in her own right. And now she was without that bit of stabilization, some concrete fantasy to keep her together. He needed to let H&B deal with this, instead of getting himself caught and getting in the way. He might make it worse by trying to do this himself.

With a breath, he turned back to the building. There was a window. There had been a window letting light in and all he had to do was look in to see if she was gone, or if they were okay. One look in a window.

He paced around the side of the building. Already he could see lights going on above him in the early morning light as people in the apartment started to rise to begin their days. He wanted to believe that whatever Willow was doing would have alerted the neighbours by now, but he couldn't count on that. He needed to make this quick, before anyone found some kid with no shoes wandering around their building. There was nothing on this side, but he knew he was very close. He rounded the corner, his heart beating hard against his ribs and feeling his lungs straining for more air as he tried to remember to breathe.

Finally, peering out the top of the very bottom of the building around the corner, he saw them. Windows. He sank immediately to his knees, seeing the room that he'd seen in his dream. Plain, tall, with the single mattress and garbage laying in one corner. It was lit better now, the day growing brighter than it had been before, and letting him see exactly what was inside.

Nothing.

He pressed his face against the glass, trying to peer in to see more. Someone should be in there. There needed to be bodies in there. He'd *seen* them. He knew they were supposed to be there. Was it the wrong room? It looked exactly like it. It *felt* just like it. He couldn't be wrong. Unless Willow was doing something, but she didn't have enough of her mind left over to do that, did she?

He was inside the room before he could stop himself, looking wildly around for anything. It was warmer in here than it was outside, but the warmth seemed contained to just his right side. When he stepped away, there was only cold. It smelled like something had burned here not long ago, but no one was here. Every corner of the room was empty. From the mattress to the walls to the small bag of garbage, no one was here. He needed *something* to be here, some sign of Max somewhere in this, but there was nothing.

Had he missed the room? This felt like the right room. It had to be.

"Max?" he asked, hearing now how short his breath was getting. It didn't matter with the sound of his heart hammering harder and harder, echoing through his head in the silence of the room. He spun around, hoping he'd missed him. Maybe he was just behind the mattress, or somewhere that he'd overlooked. "Max!"

There was a sound of something at the door and he spun to look.

Bad idea.

Harrison froze, his blood running cold. Staring back at him, red eyes looking at him curiously first, then narrowing. Willow had heard him, and had found him. His breath caught, the need to run flooding him, but he was caught in her gaze, mind devoid of places to go.

She looked like she was trying to place him, to decide what she thought of him after so long. If she even remembered him. She didn't move, though her expression grew more scrutinizing as her eyes combed over him. Her head tilted, trying to determine if there was something she should do about him.

"Hi," he breathed out after a silence. He could hear the fear in his own voice. He was sure she could hear his heart hammering, it was so loud. Memories of Adam in the hospital and the things she had done a year ago cycled through his mind. He didn't want to lose an arm. His weren't prosthetics. He needed to go. H&B needed to deal with this, not him.

Willow took a step forward and Harrison was gone, remembering his room back at the facility. It was away, it was solid, and it was nowhere near Willow. It was safe.

He pressed his back against the wall, taking some comfort in how solid it was. He didn't realize he was shaking until right then. His eyes were wide and he tried to catch his breath, finding that he wasn't alone. People were still sitting there in his room, looking like he had just intruded on their conversation. They watched him now, concern crossing their faces, though none of them tried to move forward.

"I found Willow," he managed.

CHAPTER THIRTEEN

HARRISON WASN'T SURE if he was sleeping or just laying down with his eyes closed. At least it was quiet now. Even if it had been him making most of the noise a few hours earlier.

H&B were running a skeleton staff at this hour, so there was no one he could ask to go back and get them, not that he knew where *there* was. Maya and Levi were the ones who got them back into their rooms, annoyed that they had to do anything, but making quick work of the task at hand. When Harrison couldn't give them an address and told them that he had followed a dream, they told him that they would find someone else to deal with him in the morning.

H&B would deal with this, though. He had nothing else he needed to do. In the morning, they would get all the information they needed and they would take care of everything. All he needed to do was stay put and let them handle it. They would find a way to get him to tell them where it was without him even needing to leave the building.

Everything turned over in his mind again. He knew he couldn't have been standing in front of Willow for more than five seconds, but they stretched on in his memory for hours. He couldn't really remember what she looked like except that she was familiar. Maybe a smaller version of the young woman who had watched out for them all that time ago. Other than that, not much had changed.

An address. He wished he had an address. Now, he had on pants and his charged phone firmly in his back pocket. In the morning, H&B would deal with him and he could figure out some way to tell them where it was. He could go with them and get the address and...

No, there was something wrong with that. He was supposed to stay here.

Too tired to put together what was happening in his head and too wired from what had happened to actually sleep, he let his eyes drift open to stare into the slowly growing light.

Max hadn't been there, nor had Mary. Was it the wrong room? He had never gone into the wrong place before, but lately it was happening a lot. He wondered if there was something wrong with him, or if it was something else. He couldn't know yet. As much as he didn't want to mention it, he might have to tell someone that something was going strange with his powers.

The door thumped on its hinges before it cracked open. Harrison watched as Jack let himself in and closed the door quietly behind himself. "Harrison?" he asked. Jack was trying to be quiet, but his impatience did nothing to help his volume. "You awake?"

"Yeah," he said.

He turned on the light, all attempts to be quiet gone. "What the fuck were you doing?"

Harrison sat up, letting out a sigh. He should have pretended to be asleep. "Good morning to you too," he said.

"Did you find them?"

Harrison let the question hang in the air. Jack's eyes bore into him, demanding Harrison to say what he wanted to hear. Harrison wanted to tell him just that, but he was much too tired to lie. "I thought I did," he said. "But they weren't there. Just Willow."

Jack let out a frustrated growl. He began pacing, moving back and forth around the room, his hands doing more swearing than his mouth was. "You should have brought me," he said.

"And what would you have done?"

"Kept you from running away like a little bitch until you found them!"

Harrison swung his feet over the side of the bed, keeping the desk between him and Jack. "What was the plan when Willow showed up? Punch her in the face?"

Jack turned on him, Harrison seeing the dark circles under his eyes as he stared at him. "I would have done *something!*" It was obvious that Jack wasn't doing much sleeping right now either, but Harrison didn't know how he had this kind of energy. "Take me now. We can go there right now and—"

"We should stay here," Harrison insisted. "We're no match for—"

"They're in your head, Harrison," Jack told him. "We should go for a walk. Get away from here. They keep saying things. They're planning something and I don't like it."

"They're not planning anything."

The smack echoed in the room, Harrison's face warm as the sting settled across it. He was awake now, wide eyed and on his feet. "*What is your problem?*" he demanded, shoving the table in Jack's direction.

Jack didn't move. "*Of course* they're planning something," he insisted. "You don't like these guys any more than I do. And I don't like this 'At any cost' shit Jaime's spewing. Sounds like they're okay with not getting Mary back if they can get Willow."

"But if they find Willow…"

"They're luring Willow out, Harrison," Jack snapped at him. "That doesn't sound like they're trying to find Mary to me. And I don't think—"

The door opened and Jack went silent. Emma and Jaime let themselves in, both of them looking rested and Jaime with a bag of takeout in her hands. He didn't trust it. Emma only brought him food when she wanted him to stop being a pain.

Emma turned to Jack, her hands already moving and not looking happy to see him. "If you're up, you're wanted in Lab 4," she told him.

For a moment, it looked like Jack might argue. Instead, he let out a breath, mouth closed and he nodded. He looked back to Harrison for a long moment, trying to decide what he was going to do with him before he nodded again. "Fine," he told him, heading off. "I'll see you later." It sounded like he was expecting Harrison to say something, but he left before Harrison could figure out what he was expecting.

"We brought breakfast," Jaime offered, putting the bag down on the table. Harrison could already smell the breakfast sandwich and Jaime pulled out a tray of coffees for them. "How's Willow?"

"Alive," he said. With Emma here, he signed along with his words. "Moving around. Dressed like she robbed a Hot Topic again."

"Yeah," Jaime said. "Still don't know where she got those."

"You've seen her too?"

"I've been bait for the last week," she said. She pulled up a chair and pulled out a sandwich for herself. "She stopped biting, though. Which, honestly I'm not that unhappy about. After what happened to Adam..."

"Because she knows we're onto her," Emma said. She sat down as well, pushing the bag to Harrison before she started. "Eat. We need to know exactly what happened when you decided to be a colossal idiot and went after her yourself. And you're dumb when you're tired."

"He's going to stay dumb when he's full," Jaime noted.

"Morning to you too," he said, taking a coffee. "Thanks."

"You saw Willow last night." Well, that was blunter than he was expecting, though Emma didn't look like she was in the mood to pull punches this morning. "How did you know where to go?"

"I... something happened," he said. "You probably heard about it. Jack and I, we dreamed something last night and it turned out to be real. And I just... I remembered where it was. And I went there." He shouldn't mention Tara, not yet. As uncomfortable as Tara had made him, she had helped him figure out the room he had seen. "But there wasn't anyone in there. Not at first. But then—"

"Do you know where it was?" she asked.

"No."

Emma let out a sigh and placed a sandwich in front of him. "You need to rest more, Harrison. You're not usually like this."

"I needed to see," he insisted. "It was supposed to be just a look, so I could know if I was really just dreaming or not. I know where it is, I just... I don't know. It's an apartment building. The basement. And the MAX runs past it."

"That's not really enough to go on," Emma told him. "Eat."

Obediently, Harrison picked up the sandwich. It warmed his hand, even if the egg was no longer warm in the middle of it. It tasted like something to placate him, and he found himself wanting to leave. "When are we getting out of here?"

"What do you mean?"

"We're under house arrest, right?" Harrison asked. "I mean, not like you can really do that, but you want to keep us all in one place and out of the way until you find Willow. But she's probably not coming after us. So how long are you guys going to keep us here?"

"Until we find her."

"She's not after the rest of us, Emma." The more he thought about it, the more he thought Jack was right about it. She had what she was looking for in Max and didn't look like she even really wanted Mary. She didn't even really have a place for anyone else in that room with them. "She already has what she's looking for."

"You don't know that."

"Don't I?"

"She'll come out after me," Jaime offered. "Sometimes."

"I thought you said she stopped."

"Gavin spooked her." She tossed the last of her breakfast in her mouth and chased it with a gulp of coffee. "But she did follow me around for a bit. So she's not completely ignoring us. She just doesn't want to come out here, which means we're safe in here."

"Finding her and getting her under control is top priority," Emma told him. "At any cost. As soon as we have her back, you're all free to go."

"I mean, we know *I* can leave whenever," Harrison reminded her. Jack's paranoia was starting to rub off on him and he noticed a distinct lack of follow through with this plan. "So when you get her out of wherever she is and get her back here, how are you going to find Max?"

Jaime blinked, her eyes on the table and creeping toward Emma.

Emma looked very tired. "Once she's under control, then we can get them back. We just need to get Willow back first. And to do that, we need to know where she is. You might have noticed she doesn't want to come back quietly, so we've been *trying* to surprise her. But since you were already enough of an idiot to try and track her down on your own, we need to know where you found her and make sure you haven't let her know what's going on. *If* you found her."

Harrison glared at her. "Are you saying I didn't find her?"

"I'm saying you decided to go off on your own in the middle of the night based off of a *dream*."

"I wasn't seeing things."

"Where did you find her?" Emma asked again. "We will check it out."

Harrison didn't mind Emma normally, but in this moment he didn't trust her. It didn't matter how tired he was, or that he knew that following a dream, even for them, was implausible at best. It sounded more like they were trying to retrieve their lost property than the people that property had kidnapped. And she was avoiding the question.

On the other hand, there was someone who might be able to get a straight answer out of her. His mind was already spinning, a terrible idea forming in his mind. He could feel the phone pressed into his back pocket and looked outside to see the sun fully up. She should be awake by now.

"I don't have the address," Harrison said. "I don't really know the streets here, but I can take you. Now?"

"We'll get a—"

Harrison grabbed her arm before she could protest. His hand was already in his pocket and pulling out his phone. If he wanted answers, he was going to have to move fast and hope this worked. He smiled apologetically to Jaime as they vanished.

CHAPTER FOURTEEN

EVEN THOUGH HE had no intention of getting too close to the building, it was still strange to not appear quite where he was planning. They still appeared between two buildings, but these were not the ones he was planning on. They were a block further out than he intended.

He could work with this. He had to.

His thumbs flew across his screen, unlocking his phone and he started texting. He had to do this quickly and hope that this worked. He opened his messages to find a string of texts from Tara, apologizing and asking what happened. Ignoring them, he asked her to get on the MAX and to meet him right now. He needed to figure out where this was fast, before Emma caught wind of what he was doing.

He caught a smack in the arm from Emma and immediately turned, looking innocent. "It's a couple blocks over," he told her.

"If you're going to be this reckless, why didn't you go right there?" she asked. She was clearly not happy with him, but she still followed him out onto the street, looking around and trying to get her bearings.

Harrison caught a street sign and tried to cobble together enough of a location so that Tara would know where he was. "I missed," he told her. "No big deal. There's probably nowhere hidden that we could have appeared by there anyway."

"What do you mean *you missed*?" Emma asked, her face and hands animate. "That's not how it works. You can't just *miss*."

"Apparently you can," he muttered. He spotted the sign on the intersection and sent it to Tara, seeing another text come in. Jaime wanted to know what the hell he was doing. "It's not far."

"Put down the phone, Harrison," she told him. "You don't just miss. That's not a thing that happens. What is going on?"

Harrison shook his head and pocketed his phone. He'd given Tara as much as he could for the moment. He led them down the block slowly, hoping that he would be able to stall long enough. "It's just this way," he told her, his hands bow moving with his words. "I think. I was a bit all over the place last night. It feels like it was just a little further over here."

"What do you think you're doing?"

"You needed a lead, right?" he asked. "I know where this place is, but it's not like I got the address. And you said it wasn't safe wandering around on my own, right? So here we are. And we're getting an address. And you're here to make sure Willow doesn't get her hands on me too."

As soon as he said it, he realized what a stupid plan this was, but he'd already come this far. He turned back around, trying to ignore the mounting fear that Willow was going to come out of the shadows at any moment. They made it to where he was sure she was keeping Max, back to the building with the basement windows just peeking up over the ground.

His phone went off again. He looked down to see Tara messaging him back. She was only a couple minutes away. A ghost of a smile appeared on his lips before he turned back to Emma. "It was in this building," he told her, stopping and leaning against it. "The room was empty when I looked, but Willow was down there."

"And you came here because you dreamed it?" Emma signed wildly at him. "You know this was stupid, right?"

"Come on," Harrison said. "Maybe they're in there. I might have just not seen them last night."

He led the way around the building, nerves driving him forward. He needed to see if Max was in that room now. If he was okay. He'd come so close to finding out yesterday and ran before he could be sure. Now, with Emma there, he might be able to find out if it really was all a dream.

Emma, for her part, went quiet and followed him. It felt strange to do this in the full daylight, less like he was sneaking in and more like he was planning to do something illegal later. Still, he brought her to the room with the mattress, finding it in the same condition as it had been the previous night. There was still no one inside, still only a mattress with a few bags of garbage that looked fresh. And still no sign of Max anywhere.

"They were in there?" Emma asked, peering in next to him. "You saw Willow in there?"

"Just Willow."

Emma looked from him to the window. "Stay here. I'll take a look."

Harrison looked at her right up until she vanished, catching the look on her face just before she was gone. Anger and determination. It took him a moment to remember he wasn't the only one that had to suffer whatever Willow was trying to do. Adam was still in the hospital with an arm ripped off. Fake or not, he had not looked so good without it. He wasn't the only one suffering late nights of worry from all of this.

But that wasn't going to stop him. He saw her down in the room, looking around much in the same way he had the previous night, and took out his phone. A plan. He needed to make sure there was a plan for Tara when she got here. His mind was racing as he sent a flurry of texts, trying to get his thoughts in order. This wasn't what he did. He wasn't like this. He sat down and thought things through, but there wasn't time for that right now. He was half out of his mind with worry, terrified that Willow was going to show up any moment to catch him again, or that Emma would just drag him back without talking to Tara first.

Emma vanished from the room and Harrison started moving, going to the corner by the street. Slowly, an image of what could happen fell into place. Tara was almost there. Every text sounded more ridiculous than the last, but Tara was hanging onto it, making sure she understood the plan, even if she didn't understand why.

It was stupid, but it was all he had. Either Emma found Willow and managed to get Max and Mary out of there, or Tara would be here to make sure he got his answers. Or Willow would show up and he didn't know what was going to happen to him. If that happened, well, none of this would really matter anymore.

He stared around the corner, watching the traffic and the MAX as it kept going by. There were two stops, and neither of them had Tara getting off of them. Soon. She said she was almost there. They just needed to not be gone before she got there.

The tap on his shoulder made him jump out of his skin, his phone dropping out of his hands and onto the concrete. He spun back around, finding Emma looking at him worried and like she was trying to keep a small puppy calm. "Just me," she told him. "No one's in there."

He blinked at her. He didn't like that answer, but that did give him a better idea of what to do next. "No one?"

Emma shook her head. "It looks like they were in there once. Or someone was. Willow was, definitely, and other people. But they aren't there anymore. We need to get someone else in, someone who can do more than I can."

Time. He needed more time. They couldn't go yet. Tara was almost here. "Max isn't there?"

"No one's in there anymore," she repeated. "We should go back."

"They might come back."

"I believe you that they were there," she told him slowly. She tried to step away from the street and somewhere quieter where they could disappear, but Harrison stayed where the cars passing by could clearly see them. Where Tara would be able to spot them. "But they aren't there anymore. They're gone."

"They can't just be gone," he insisted. "It's not like Mary would have gone willingly with whatever Willow wanted to do."

"Harrison, calm down. We need to head back."

"Is it because I went in?" he asked, already knowing that was the answer. He was familiar enough with how this worked. It was standard procedure when they were traveling with Luke and Willow. If they were found, they were immediately moved. It hadn't occurred to him before, but now that he thought about it, it made perfect sense. He missed the room and Willow probably moved them immediately. "I shouldn't have gone in."

"No. You shouldn't have. But it's too late to change that now." She looked tired and like she might grab him, but she was aware of just how many people would see. " Come on, we'll just head back. Get reinforcements and we'll come back and look at it again."

"You mean *you* will," Harrison snapped back. "I'll be stuck back there again."

"It's safer for you."

"Harrison!"

The sound of Tara's voice was a welcome relief. For a moment, he'd forgotten what he was trying to do here. He wanted answers, and Emma was going to give them to him, one way or another. He hoped Tara could remember everything.

"Hey," he said. There was a plan. He could do this. He forced himself to straighten up, like nothing of the last conversation had happened. "Hey, um," he said, looking back at Emma, then to Tara, "Emma, Tara," he said. His words were getting mixed in his head. The plan was too loose and he was doubting it, but there was nothing left but to follow through with it now. "Tara is a friend of Max's. Emma's looking into what happened to him."

Tara seemed to know her part much better than Harrison did, stepping past him with a hand outstretched and curiosity in her eyes. "Hi," she said, the smile on her lips doing nothing to erase the worry in her eyes. "I can't believe Max is gone again. Do you know what happened to him? I mean, you're going to be able to get him back again, right?"

Emma hesitated, glancing back to Harrison. He nodded, understanding what was happening here. When Emma let go of Tara's hand, her hands started moving. Tara stepped back, surprise on her face and shame in her eyes as she looked from Emma to Harrison.

Right. He didn't mention this part.

"I'm so sorry," Tara said. "I just— I don't know, I didn't know, I—"

"It's okay," Harrison said, echoing what Emma was already saying. "I got this. Just..." he motioned for her to pay attention to Emma, stepping aside to act as translator.

"We can't say anything about what's happening right now," Emma said. "We are doing everything we can to find them and bring them back."

For her part, Tara only glanced at Harrison once as Emma told her what he thought was a far too standard answer. Tara watched her curiously and Harrison could hear the bit of static itching into the back of his mind. Now that he was looking for it, it was easy to pick up on. He hoped Emma would miss it.

"Is it like last time?" Tara asked, keeping her eyes on Emma and her voice down. They moved off to the side so people could walk past, out of the way as Tara tried to press. "He got kidnapped again, didn't he?"

"Yes."

"By different people this time, right?"

"One of the same people as last time." A sour expression formed on Emma's face. "But we're going to find her. And I'm going to make sure she doesn't do it again."

Harrison wondered how much of that was Tara managing to pull it out of her and how much was Emma letting her fatigue and worry spill over.

"She's not coming after Harrison too, is she?" Tara asked, wide eyed. "Or Ted? Like, is she going to get them all again?"

Emma shook her head, Harrison trying not to look surprised at that. "She doesn't want them. They're not going to be any use to her. We haven't quite figured out why she even took Mary. The only one she really wants is Max."

"Why?"

This is where Emma faltered, like she realized something was wrong. Harrison shot Tara a sharp look, silently hoping she understood.

"So Harrison's out here helping you find him?" Tara asked. Slowly, Harrison could see the realization of what she was being called here for dawning on her face. She was finally starting to realize what she was doing to people.

"Harrison had a lead," Emma told her. "It's gone cold."

"So if you're done with him, mind if we head off for some breakfast?" Tara asked. "You can come too. There's a great place for waffles about a block from here."

"We need to head back. We shouldn't even be out here in the first place."

"Aw, why?"

"Because H&B needs to keep them out of the way."

"Out of the way? Of what?"

"If it comes down to it, the priority is Willow," Emma told her. "And H&B has decided that they will be a liability if they were allowed to interfere. Though," Emma added, glancing at Harrison, "I don't know that it's the best idea. Harrison and Jack are the only ones who have been able to find them so far."

"You're going to get them back alive, right?"

"It depends on who finds them. And if they get in the way."

Emma stopped very suddenly as she finished saying that, her hands frozen in the air and her back very straight. Her eyes very slowly looked Tara over and Harrison knew she had caught on. She kept her shoulders square and tapped Harrison on the arm, nodding for the two of them to leave.

"We have to get going," he said, feeling shaken but trying to keep it together. "Text me tonight?"

She nodded and Harrison let himself be led away by Emma. Her grip on his arm was a lot stronger than usual and he wondered if perhaps he'd gone too far. Still, his heart was racing as he tried to process the new information and decide what he should do next.

"Who is she?" Emma asked finally when they were alone.

"A friend of Max's," Harrison said. "Best friend. She lives next door. They grew up together."

Emma considered this, but softened finally. "Look. I don't like this either. But the best way to get Max back is to figure out where he is sooner than later. So if you have any leads or any other dreams, tell me first and don't go looking yourself. We can't keep scaring Willow off before there's a chance."

Harrison nodded, taking a deep breath. He wasn't sure he would be able to follow that, knowing that all it took was the wrong people going in to make Max staying alive no longer a priority. At the very least, he'd gotten his answers. He let Emma take him back, though he was already trying to come up with another course of action the next time he had one of those dreams.

CHAPTER FIFTEEN

MOST OF THE thoughts Harrison managed on his own were about how this was probably completely pointless and only intended to keep him from going anywhere. Devlyn kept his mind filled with static and unable to come up with another location, keeping him there to try and do whatever it was that Gethen asked until he was content that he couldn't do any of it.

At least he knew to stay quiet in his failure.

"This is fucking stupid," Jack told Gethen. His eyes were bloodshot and Harrison could see the redness in his face flushing red, making the white of his scars stand out stronger than before. "What do you think I'm going to do? I'm going to suddenly be able to read minds?"

A smile stayed across Gethen's face. He looked on in amusement as he circled around behind Jack, looking down on him like a particularly troublesome pet he was fond of. "You've already shown some promise," he said. "A dream of where they were. But a dream isn't quite as useful to me as a *location*."

"You can't keep us in here," Jack hissed. He planted his hands on the table, trying to push himself up.

"Actually, I can. See, you have all broken our little agreement. It's been determined that your recklessness and habit of getting caught by civilians means that you are no longer permitted civilian lives. Which means I get to stop taking it quite so easy on you."

"There's no way you—"

Gethen smiled even wider. Not so gently, he tapped Devlyn on the head.

Across from him, Jack doubled over. Harrison averted his eyes back down to the map between them, feeling Devlyn getting louder. Jack groaned as he pushed himself back up, but Gethen only laughed. "Now concentrate," he said, taking a little too much joy in how Jack growled back at him. "That girlfriend of yours didn't get along too well with her, did she? If you want her back, one of you will need to find them."

He didn't even know how this was supposed to work. He couldn't even teleport based on a map, so how were they supposed to be able to pinpoint anything on here? The static was certainly doing something to his mind, but he didn't think it was making it any better at developing a connection to Max so much as it was keeping him from being able to tell where he was.

Gethen looped back around to Devlyn and rapped her hard once more on the back of the head, but this time the static came to an abrupt halt. It was followed by a crash as Devlyn fell face first onto the ground, stiff and not moving.

Silence followed it. Harrison stared down at her, trying to figure out what had happened. He'd knocked her on the head plenty of times so far, and it had been followed by no response from her. He didn't appear to have done anything differently, but she was not moving. He couldn't even see the rise and fall of her back. She might not be breathing.

Gethen let out a deep sigh that echoed in the small room. "Well then," he said. "I suppose you're both free to go until we can find another one."

Harrison glanced back to Jack, trying to see if he knew what had just happened. He wanted to go to Devlyn, to see if she was all right, but he could almost hear Jack telling him that they needed to get out of there. If he did that to one of the Keepers, then there was no telling what was going to happen to them if they stayed for much longer and didn't give him the results he wanted.

———◆———

HARRISON SAT ON his bed with his head resting against the wall, staring up at the ceiling and wondering when the last of the static was going to finally disperse from his mind. He felt fine some moments, while the world rocked in others. Ally had taken over the desk again, taking their house arrest as a time to get ahead on classes that she was going to pass anyway while Jack stared at books and frowned.

"How long have we even been here?" Jack asked, finally closing his books and placing a sandwich on top of them. He sounded less tired, but he looked like he could collapse any moment as well. "You know, we ate better when we were on the run than in here."

"About a week," Ally said. She didn't sound sure, though that might have been a response to whatever code she was currently tinkering with. "What are they doing to you in there?"

"Useless shit." Jack started taking the sandwich apart, removing the onions from the middle, followed by everything else he didn't like. "Where's Jaime? She should have to suffer in here like the rest of us."

"She's working. I don't know what you're so mad about. It's not like you had anything else to do anyway. You're not even doing *your own* work. You're just..." She glanced at him and stopped as she caught a look at his plate and the pickles now sitting on top of the pile of onions. "Are you really still that picky?"

Jack glared at her, not breaking eye contact as he took a bite of his sandwich. "Why are *you* still in here?"

"So Willow doesn't come after me?"

"She's not coming after you," Harrison said, watching Ally. He was pretty sure Jaime said that she no longer worked as bait for Willow, so he wasn't sure what she was working on anymore. "They're just keeping us here to keep us out of the way."

"And how do you know that?" Ally asked slowly, eyes inching away from the discards of Jack's sandwich and slowly over to Harrison. Jack was less subtle.

"Asked Emma."

"And why did *she* tell you?"

"Trade secret," Harrison told her. "H&B think we're going to get in the way of getting Willow back. They don't even care if they get Max and Mary back."

"That's not *completely* true," Ted said, appearing at the door. "Have you guys thought about maybe hanging out in one of the parts of this place with couches or literally anywhere else? I've been trying to find you."

"Try texting next time."

"I did. You guys didn't pick up."

Harrison pulled his phone out of his pocket to check the battery, but that wasn't the problem. There was no reception; he had missed a message from Tara. He let that sit there, not bothering to check it as he pocketed his phone once more. He was pretty sure his phone had worked in here before.

Ally frowned at him and hit a few keys on her laptop before closing it. "We're always in here."

"But do we *have* to be?" Ted asked, taking a seat on the floor by the bed. "The static's driving me kind of crazy."

"The what?"

"No, go back," Jack insisted, looking back to Harrison. "What do you mean they aren't trying to get Mary back? If they aren't even doing *that*—"

"I mean, they still want to get them back too," Ted said. "Maybe just— look, so I've been bored. And I don't go hard on homework like Ally. So I went to check out a few things, and I found out why they had Willow here. Mary was supposed to be in for a week for testing, right? Like, next week?"

"Yeah...."

"So Max was showing better results so far, so they brought him in first. They kept Willow in the room next door and wanted to see if he would get unlocked. That's what they call it. They were trying to get him to be like the rest of them. Like Adam and Emma and all the Keepers. They can do all these other things, and they've been trying to figure out how to get the rest of us to do the same."

"Yeah, the Keepers can do that because of *torture*," Jack said. "Have they been fucking *torturing* people?"

The world was moving again. Harrison closed his eyes, waiting for it to stop.

"You've seen Mary when she gets out of a longer run in here, right?" Ted asked. "And Max is worse."

"How do you torture someone into superpowers?" Ally asked.

"Do you not know this?" Jack demanded. "*You were there last year.* I wasn't even there and *I* know this! How do you *not* know this? You *do* know Max, right?"

"It's not like I talk to him about how people got *tortured!*"

"*Guys!*" Ted snapped, trying to calm them down. "Can't you guys at least cool it until I finish telling you what's going on? I'm barely even started."

"They got electrocuted so much they can't talk anymore!"

"Enough, Jack!" Harrison snapped. He missed Mary's ability to keep Jack from going overboard, and it looked like Ted was feeling much the same. "You can tell her all about it later. Ted found out why the hell Willow is even here."

Ted waited until he had everyone's attention before he continued. "Okay, so while they were transferring Adam back in, I slipped into— that part isn't important," he said quickly, glancing up to the corner of the room.

"Max said that one doesn't work anymore," Harrison told him. He closed his eyes and let his head rest back against the wall again, letting out a breath as a wave of dizziness hit him. Max had stuck a bit of paper onto it at some point that Harrison could not get off. While he was trying, he was sure to accidentally break the microphone.

Still, Ted lowered his voice and turned away from the camera. "So they *really* want us to be able to be like all the Keepers," he repeated. "And at this facility, Max and Mary were the two closest."

"You did this part," Jack snapped.

"And at the end," Ted said, "Max was starting to do it. He was starting to move things and they were trying to figure out if some of the other stuff was him actually doing stuff with the water around him or just an extension of that. There was a note where he might have set something on fire, but Kenzie nearby, so they aren't really sure about that one. They were planning to bring him in again after Mary to do it again."

"Maybe they just needed to set him on fire…" Jack started, but the sharp glare from Ally cut him short.

"Thing is, they needed to send him home a little early. They were watching Willow too, and there was something weird happening with her. They weren't sure what it was, but when Max left, she seemed to go back to normal. They thought she did, anyway. Until she went and broke out of here."

"Did Max happen to mention to you that he could suddenly move shit with his mind?" Jack asked.

Ted shook his head. "I called him in the morning when I found out he got out early. He was just stressing out about Harrison the whole time. I don't think he even remembered the last bit of being in there. It was like that had happened yesterday to him, but he was in there for at least another day after he sent you back home. I don't really know what the timing was, but..."

Harrison opened his eyes and looked up at the ceiling. "And then Willow decided to go and grab both of them." The more he learned about H&B, the less he trusted them, but he didn't know where else to go right now. If he could figure out how to get Max away from Willow without her catching the two of them, he'd do it himself, but the thought of facing her again terrified him. He didn't want to end up in the hospital.

But he also wanted to get Max back. And for the world to stop taking sudden dips around him.

"Where's Jaime?" Ted asked. "Gavin was looking for her. Shouldn't she be stuck in here with us too?"

"Apparently she gets to leave if she's doing H&B's bidding," Jack said, slamming his hands onto the table and sticking his fingers in the plate of discarded onions. "The rest of us broke contract so we can't go anywhere."

"*I* didn't do anything," Ally pointed out. "I'm sure they'll let me out."

Jack laughed at her, shaking his head like she was a delusional child that he didn't want to bother correcting. "We need to get out of here. We can find them ourselves."

Ally looked pointedly down at the plate, then back to him. "*How?* You aren't in any condition to go anywhere right now,

Jack. And you don't know where they are! You don't even know where to start looking!"

"We go back to the same place! We know where they were last; we just take it from there."

"And how are you getting there?"

"We *have* a teleporter. H&B can't do shit to make him stay here."

"If you think I can get this many people anywhere right now, you are mistaken," Harrison told him, closing his eyes tight.

"Stop being such a bitch and—"

"You need to calm your ass down!" Ally snapped back at him.

Ted stood up and tried to get between them. "You *both* need to calm down!"

"Why don't you set me on fire again?" Jack dared her. "See if I suddenly figure out how to teleport myself."

"You know every single one of us could leave whenever we wanted," Harrison pointed out. "There is literally nothing keeping us here. For example."

Harrison didn't have a plan for where to go when he vanished, his mind turning over what he did know. Willow had Max. He had no idea where Max was. But there was something about where he had ended up that sounded a bit like him.

He sagged heavily against the wall and let himself drop down to the ground, already feeling a headache coming from the exertion of the testing today. He hadn't eaten since the morning and now his mind was turning over and over again, which gave him a distraction from what his stomach was doing.

He knew they were keeping him tired, but there wasn't anything else to do. Jaime was the only one allowed to go out and do anything right now, so long as she had Gavin keeping an eye out on her as she tried to lure Willow out into the open. Except that she wasn't working as bait anymore. Maybe H&B would decide to try roping one of the rest of them into this.

A sound hit his ears and he looked up. Static. What had Ted said? That the static was driving him crazy? Harrison could hear it in his head since Doctor Gethen had failed to use him as a human GPS tracker, but this was the first time he'd actually heard anything like it. Somehow, it still sounded a bit familiar, and it was almost calling to him.

He forced himself to his feet and stumbled forward, his hand pressing against the wall on the other side of the dark hall. He should figure out where he was first, but there was something strange about it. He should run. He knew he would normally want him to run, but whatever was on the other side sounded like Max and like he needed help. And he knew Max was in desperate need of help right now.

The room was dark inside when he appeared on the other side of the door, though that wasn't the first thing that hit him. The first thing was the sound from the speaker, much louder on this side. It drove something into his mind and suffocated him. This was a bad idea, he knew it as soon as he looked around, but he knew it was too late for him.

The faint light of the machinery showed him a few beds in the room, but it was hard to concentrate on any of that when it felt like his brain was trying to melt out of his ears. He pressed his palms over the side of his head, trying to block out the sound, but his legs were too weak to keep him up. Desperately, he looked around, trying to remember where the door was, only to find himself looking at another bed.

Oh. There was Jaime.

And there was the floor.

CHAPTER SIXTEEN

"COME ON, MAX. Hang in there. Just stay with me."

Mary's voice sounded so far away, but Max still tried to drag himself closer to it. He couldn't even feel his limbs, and what he could feel of himself either tingled or felt like it was unravelling bit by bit. The closer to Mary he got, the more real he felt. The more of his body came back, the more pain he was in. He could feel the knives in his throat as his dragged each shallow breath into his lungs, and he thought that maybe going back to Mary was not the best idea.

Something else thought it was a very good idea for him to just stay down as well. Something he was starting to realize wasn't him. Something he needed to disobey as much as possible. Something else right there with him. Something that terrified him.

Slowly, Mary's voice got clearer and closer. She kept her voice low, the rasp in it showing her own fatigue. Max could feel her hand on his head, gently stroking his hair as he rested in her lap.

Slowly his eyes flitted open, looking up to see she wasn't even looking at him. Her head rested against the wall and she stared at nothing. Even in the low light, he could see the bruises decorating her arms and blooming on her neck. "You aren't leaving me here alone, Max," she continued. "You stay here. Stay with me, Max."

Max tried to say something, but all that came out was a strangled groan. Mary looked down, her hand clamping down hard over mouth and gripping his face hard. Her attention snapped down to him, eyes wide and alert as they combed over him.

"Good," she said, looking relieved. Her shoulders relaxed and she let her hand fall off of his mouth to his collar. Her hand was relaxed, but he could tell she had a finger resting on his pulse. The haze in his head lightened as he realized Mary was trying to pull herself in. Max wasn't even sure how much of the fuzz flooding his mind was his own, but it was getting easier to think. "No more scaring me like that."

Max dragged in another breath, letting his head sag into a nod. He wasn't trying to scare her. He didn't know what was actually happening; only that Willow seemed very intent on electrocuting him at every chance she had. He was almost certain his heart had stopped a few times now, and he was feeling more and more weak every time she decided she wanted to see him. He didn't know what she wanted, or he would have already given it to her.

"Talk to me Max," Mary told him. "Let me know you're here."

"Do I have to be?" He could hear how weak his own voice was and he swallowed hard against the feeling in his throat. He needed water and several other things. A sense of what was up and down, for one thing, instead of this constant dizziness. He needed his thoughts to clear, for the fuzz and static overtaking his thoughts to leave him alone and let him figure out what was going on. He needed to know where he was and how to get out of here. At the very least, he needed Mary to get out of here before she got any more hurt than she already was.

His thoughts flickered to Harrison, but he didn't want him here. He didn't want anyone anywhere near here.

"Yes," Mary told him. She relaxed under him, resting her head back against the wall and staring once more at nothing. "You stay here."

The haze in his head pushed back, making his breath catch in his throat in a wheeze. Mary tensed against his neck as Max tried to return his breathing to normal, to push back the wave of dizziness that followed. His head started to throb in a slow rhythm, promising to turn to a pounding shortly. "Don't wanna…"

"I don't like what happens when you go away, Max," Mary told him. "You need to stay here from now on."

He couldn't figure out what she was talking about, but it didn't matter when breathing and talking were this hard. He looked up at the ceiling, feeling like he'd stared at this ceiling before. He looked back to Mary, blinking slowly and trying to make his eyes focus on something. Staying here, as it turned out, was getting harder by the moment. "No promises."

His eyes slid slowly closed and open again. Breathing was getting easier, but it was still a chore. His limbs, now that he could feel them again, all throbbed and tingled like they might fade away again. Max wasn't sure that was a bad thing. Even his eyes felt strange as he took in the room, growing more and more sure as he looked at the walls that he had been here before.

"Keep talking," Mary insisted. "Let me know you're still here, Max."

"I know this place." The look of the ceiling he knew. The room had been rearranged, the paint no longer pink on the walls, but he remembered this room. The fairy lamp was still there, offering no light at the moment. He bit down on the doll as he tried to get his bone straight. There was plastic so he wouldn't bleed on anything. "They took us here. Before. I've been here before."

"You knew the last one too," Mary told him. "And you knew we would be coming here next."

"The next one will be... blue?" he continued, barely registering what she said. He knew what was going on. At least, he remembered the houses. What was going on, he didn't really know. "A blue room. Adjoining bathroom. And then the one with a pool. And then the empty one."

"Do you remember the last one, Max?" she asked. "Do you remember the last room? The one we were in before this one?"

He thought for only a moment. "No," he told her. The last one he really remembered was the room with the windows too high to reach. He knew there had been others, but the details were fuzzy, and clouded with red eyes and pain. Even now, it was hard to keep any thoughts in order. He could only really focus on what was happening right now. There was dread, but he couldn't quite remember what he was afraid of. But he knew it was coming and there was nothing he could do to stop it.

No. It wasn't just coming. It was...

He took in another breath, the fuzz in his mind getting heavier. It felt foreign, but Mary looked too calm to be doing it. Sometimes she was like that, calm on the outside and fuming on the inside, but she didn't usually look so tired. "You okay?" he asked. He should get up from her lap, but everything hurt to move. "You look bad. Are things..." He couldn't come up with a better word, struggling to even keep his focus this much. He'd go with it. Mary would understand. "Are things happening?"

"You figured it out last time," she told him. "Willow is taking us to the gate. She's going to throw me in to open it. Just like Sarah. I should be honoured." Her voice was distant, like she had already accepted that it was going to happen. She sounded so tired. So distant.

He was drifting away. Max tried to keep himself there. Something was pulling him away and he tried to hold on to Mary's voice. But she'd stopped talking, and this other static that filled his mind felt so soothing. Like if he went away into it, he wouldn't hurt anymore. And he didn't want to hurt anymore.

"Max," came Mary's voice. "Keep talking Max. Let me know you're still here. Stay with me, Max."

But Mary was there. And he couldn't leave Mary alone. Not when she was asking him to stay. "Here," he said, though he didn't know what else to say. It was taking more effort now to stay there when there was something else pulling him so gently away.

"We'll get out of this, Max," she told him. "You still need to talk to Harrison."

"Harrison..."

"The nice boy whose heart you broke," she told him. She sounded stronger now. At least, she sounded more like her old self. And underlining her words, something else lingered where Max couldn't grasp it. "You need to tell him you're sorry."

The face came back. A calming face. At least he wasn't here. As much as he would have preferred Harrison's company, he never wanted to see him in the same condition Mary was in right now. It was almost good the way it had happened, even if it made his insides hurt as much as his outsides. "We broke up."

"You're going to un-break up," Mary told him. "And then you'll go back to being insufferable again."

"We're not that bad."

"You're disgusting," Mary pressed, rapping a finger against his neck. "It's going to be so much worse when you actually start saying *boyfriend* to people."

"Harrison can find someone who will do that now."

"You aren't getting off that easy. You still need to talk to him, Max."

"We might not get out of here." The haze over his mind was getting stronger again, that thing pulling him away. He could feel another something in the room with them, but maybe it was Mary. She was getting more annoyed. It might be Mary.

Mary gave him a flick to his forehead and Max winced. Frowning, she pat the spot, rubbing it soothingly. "We're getting out, Max," she told him firmly, though he could tell she didn't believe it. "And then you're talking to him. You owe him at least that."

He owed him a lot more than that. Harrison deserved a boyfriend that didn't end up in these situations that made him worry so much. One who didn't get stressed up and break up with him by accident. Multiple times. One that didn't send him away and possibly screwed up his brain while doing so to the point that he needed to send someone to make sure he was okay.

One who could actually introduce him to friends as his boyfriend.

"Stay here Max."

One who could stay here instead of letting himself continuously drift away into a place where he was in less pain and where nothing else seemed to matter as much. Max dragged himself back again. It was getting harder and harder every time. It was like someone else wanted him to go away. "Is there someone else here?"

Mary went very still. "No, Max," she told him firmly. "No one else. Just you and me."

"I can hear someone else," he told her.

"Push him back, Max," Mary told him. He could hear something creeping into her voice. Uneasiness and fear. She knew what was happening. "There's no one else here but us, Max. Just stay... Stay with me. And stay down."

Mary moved under him, taking his head off of her lap and lowering it onto the floor. A moment later, he felt it too, somewhere in that other static. Something else was coming. Mary used the wall to get to her feet, standing in front of him as he let his head drop to the side. He watched her feet and the floor beyond them.

Willow clad in a black dress and a curious expression appeared in the room. She was more amused than anything, watching Mary like a disobedient child and waiting to see what she would try today.

Max didn't have enough of his head together to even be scared, though his breathing hitched as he realized what this meant. Pain was coming. A lot of it. That other thing in his head soothed him, assuring him if he just drifted away he wouldn't have to deal with any of that.

Move.

Neither Willow's lips or hands moved, but Max could hear her voice nestled in his ears and echoing back into his mind, louder than if she had actually spoken. Mary wasn't as clear as she was.

"Make me," Mary said. "You can't keep doing this, Willow. He's not here anymore. He's dead. All you're doing is killing Max. And it's *just* Max. No one else. Luke is dead and he's not coming back."

Her words were both strange and incredibly familiar. Max knew he'd heard her say something like this before, somewhere in another house, standing much like this, but the ideas behind the words felt foreign. Luke was dead. He knew Luke was dead. But the haze and the static in his head was only getting stronger the closer Willow got, like it wanted to see her. Like it was still alive. Like it wanted out.

Like it was Luke.

I said move.

"I said no."

It didn't matter how firm Mary tried to hold her spot. She was in the air a moment later, slamming into the roof of the house in the middle of the room so hard that drywall rained down around him. Mary let out a low groan above him, clearly trying to bite back something stronger. Max saw her try to pull away, watched as Willow's steps slowed as she drew slowly closer to Max.

"He's dead!" Mary yelled at her. "Luke is dead! That's just Max! Back off of—"

A heavy clunk stopped Mary's speech, followed by the sound of her falling back down to the ground. She was a heap, not moving from her spot on the carpet. Max tried to do anything and his muscles screamed as he forced his arms to move. He fell back into his mind and into that other static. The pain in his body as he tried to pull himself to Mary helped to keep him there. He needed to see if Mary was all right. She needed to be alright. He was supposed to stay with her. That meant she needed to stay with him too.

He didn't get far before he was reminded very sharply of how futile anything they tried to do was. Willow was there, not paying Mary any mind as she stepped over her. She knelt down in front of Max, looking him over with those scrutinizing red eyes. The desire to run overtook him, though physically he could not. He only had his head to retreat into now, and that wasn't far enough away to escape those red eyes that would haunt his nightmares. If he had nightmares.

Come on. Willow looked like this was only a minor annoyance as she poked him sharply in the forehead.

His body let out a strangled gasp as the current flooded through him. Any hold he had on being present fell away into the buzzing in his ears. The numbness and agony returned and it was everything. Max drifted further, away from the pain and away from Willow. Mary would be mad, but he couldn't handle it anymore. He didn't want to be in pain. That haze, that static promised that he would be safe if he just retreated back into it. The other static would take care of it. Everything would be fine.

From very far away, Max felt his body move without him, getting to its feet while barely moving any of the muscles in his legs. His body was limp, but something moved him, putting him on his feet, making the head he couldn't hold up look forward. It all felt so distant and far away, but out there, he heard his voice speak.

"Hey, Will. Let's see how long he stays quiet this time."

CHAPTER SEVENTEEN

HARRISON WAS VAGUELY aware of movement. It might have been him moving. He wasn't sure. His entire being was comprised mostly of static and he was only just familiar with the idea that anything else existed. He wasn't even sure if he was awake, or if those sounds around him were real. He was starting to feel warm. Something bright came into existence. The smell of fire surrounded him. The air might be getting thicker. His lungs were coming back to him and they did not much like what was going into them.

He might be imagining everything. Might still be unconscious. Might be dreaming.

There was something on his face. Hands. Fingers prying his eyes open and hands slapping him hard in the face. Flecks of water and hot breath. Morning breath in his face, filling his nostrils and trickling into his lungs. Words forcing their way loudly into his ears, though his brain was having trouble making sense of them. *Up,* the words insisted. *Harrison.*

He knew the words, though it took a very long time for them to make sense. He knew the second one. That was his name. His brain rattled and he realized something was shaking him between hard smacks to the face. Yelling at him. Something urgent was happening and something needed him to get up. His head felt too heavy, still stuffed full of cotton, but whatever they wanted was important. He should at least try to come around and find out what they wanted.

"Harrison I swear to god I will throw you in the fire if you don't *wake the hell up!*"

He knew the person shaking him. Jack. That person was Jack. His eyes cracked open amidst the shaking and he could see the blurry shape of him devouring what little vision he had. He couldn't open them any further, but he could make out that jawline and the mouth so close to his face that Harrison thought he might bite him if he didn't do what he was asked.

"Calm down. He probably can't even hear you."

Female voice. He knew that one too, though it took longer to place Ally. She was another one of the blurs, probably. There were a few blurs, some of them bigger and some of them smaller, and he didn't know what to make out of any of them. They sounded nervous. Or angry. Maybe both. The haze over his mind was so thick and heavy that it was hard to make out any of it. Too heavy to get him to open his eyes any further.

Something was happening. He knew he didn't like all this shaking, but he didn't know how to stop it. Everything kept moving around. The light kept changing. The static in his head was almost painful as it started to retreat and he didn't know what he was supposed to do. He should try to move away from all this shaking and smacking, but he couldn't quite put together how. He could barely even open his eyes right now, could barely breathe with the weight on his chest.

"And how long you think setting the door on fire is going to keep them off? Harrison, get us the hell out of here!"

The fresh bout of shaking wasn't helping, but he roughly knew what he was supposed to do now to make it stop. They wanted to leave. He didn't know where they wanted to go, but he didn't know where other places were at the moment either. He could get them away. All of them. Whoever they were. However many of them. There were other voices, other shapes that were probably people moving around him. They all wanted to leave. They had to go away.

Away. They would go away.

IT WAS HOURS later when Harrison finally opened his eyes. There was a noise that had brought him back around, but whatever it had been, it was gone now, but it was not quiet. His head was no longer filled with a heavy haze, instead being weighed down by an all-encompassing headache, his nostrils filled with a sour tang of something going bad. He groaned, already regretting consciousness, and rolled over to his side to see if there was anything keeping him from just going back to sleep.

There was blood on the floor and the walls, but he knew this room. They had been here not long ago. They were back in Mary and Jack's apartment, the bed now back in place so Harrison could sleep on it. Outside, he could hear voices muffled by the closed door, none of them sounding like they were trying to be quiet. He recognized all of them, at least, and none of them made him think he was in immediate danger.

He tried to close his eyes once more, but the throbbing in his head only grew with every moment he was awake. His stomach turned, demanding something to fill it now that he was conscious again. His face stung and throbbed. Reluctantly, he rolled over onto his back and covered his face with an arm. There would be no more sleep for the moment at least.

Okay. What was going on?

He remembered going into the room. He remembered blacking out from the weight of everything. He sort of remembered waking up, and he was pretty sure that was why his face felt so strange. Gently he touched one of his cheeks, almost certain there was going to be a bruise fully formed there soon enough. He let out a slow breath, trying to get his head clear enough, though he couldn't put together what had happened in there, or what had brought them here. Somehow, they got here. And he might have gotten them out of the facility, but he doubted he had gotten them all the way out here on his own.

And, of course, there was what he'd seen while he was out cold. Already his heart felt tight in his chest. He couldn't be sure about what he'd seen. He knew that it was real, that it had happened, but there was nothing he could do about it at this moment. Right now, he needed to figure out what was going on.

He could still feel his phone pressing into his back pocket and took it out. He had missed messages from just about everyone over the past while, it seemed, though he ignored them. His sister was worried, but there was nothing he could do about it. His thumbs moved across the small screen, sending a quick message to let her know that she probably wouldn't see him for a while.

With a sigh, he knew it was time to face whatever was happening. The bed creaked under him as he pushed himself up, the sound doing nothing to help the pounding in his head. Outside, everything went quiet as he got to his feet. He stumbled until he reached the wall and leaned on it for support until he was stable. He felt like he hadn't moved in days, his limbs stiff and joints resisting every movement. Gingerly, he got to the door and went to the living room.

It wasn't quite the scene he was expecting. Yes, Jack was looking sullen on one side of the room and Ally looked like she was still fuming. Jaime appeared to be nursing her own head-ache on the chair, but Ted was in the middle of it all with parts from something spread out wide across the living room. Jack was glaring at Ted specifically, though Ted was much more con-cerned with his screwdriver and whatever he was assembling on the coffee table. Or disassembling.

"How are you feeling?" Ted asked, not looking up.

"Like crap," Harrison said. "What happened?"

"You were a dumbass and disappeared for three days," Ally snapped at him.

"We broke out," Jack continued over top of her. "They had you and Jaime locked away and knocked out. Couldn't wake you up no matter what we tried to do."

"And that's why my face hurts."

"You weren't waking up."

Harrison shook his head, going to drop next to Ted on the couch and took a deep breath. Standing was too much of a chore, and he let his head sink into his hands as he drew in a long breath. The pain in his head wasn't going away yet and he was no closer to figuring out what happened. Slow-ly, he tried to piece together what little he could make his brain put together on its own. "So we're running from H&B, right?"

"Right."

"And you really think they aren't going to look for us here?"

"Well, you didn't get us very far," Jack informed him. He sounded like he was trying to not sound too accusatory and failing. "There's only so far we could go with two unconscious people on our backs before they found us again, you know."

"It's a miracle he got us out at all," Ted said, putting down the screwdriver and letting whatever project was scattered across the room sit. "I'm getting nowhere on this. Ally, you got any ideas?"

"How about drop it?" Jack offered.

"How about you shut up for five minutes?" Ally snapped at him. She brought a cup over, shoving it into Harrison's hands before dropping down on Ted's other side. "You need to give me more of a rundown on how this thing works before I can help, Ted."

"What is that thing?" Harrison asked. He was getting no answers, though he wasn't entirely certain what his questions were right now either.

"That's the thing that knocked us out," Jaime told him, her voice pained and quiet. He looked over, seeing her head also resting in her hand and curled up on the chair. He felt the same way and was glad that she wasn't as loud as everyone else right now. And like she was going to actually tell him what he was looking for if he asked.

"What happened?" he asked. He took a seat at the other end of the couch, bringing his legs up and resting his back against the arm rest.

She shook her head, but didn't look up. "I went looking for more information after you disappeared with Emma," she told him. "They told me and Gavin something different. And they moved Adam in without telling anyone, so I thought I'd see why. I tried asking and they took me to see Adam. That was the last thing I knew until we got here. Near as I've gotten out of the arguing, they went looking for you and got caught when they shut that thing off. And they brought it with them when they got out."

"I think there was something about a fire too," Harrison told her, vaguely recalling that.

"Oh, so you were awake after all," Jack said, sounding irritated.

"I also remember a lot of slapping and shaking," Harrison added, venom in his words. "You know anything about that?"

Jack looked like he was about to say something, but Ally was quick to chime in. "We got caught," she said. "And we needed to get out. It's not like we could just run out of there. You don't remember getting us out of there?"

"Kind of. My head still feels like there's cotton in it."

"That's the machine," Ted told him. "It's supposed to make it seem like... you know when Max and Mary get really stressed out? That thing that happens? It does that to you. They managed to find exactly the frequency for it where it only affects us, but not anyone else."

"I am suddenly very happy this thing is in pieces."

"It's not staying in pieces," Ted said. "I'm figuring out how this works and I'm making it portable."

"*Why*?" Jack demanded. It didn't sound like it was the first time.

"Because if Maya or Levi show up to try and take us back in, or if you two figure out where Willow is, we're going to need something more useful than *us* against them," Ted told him. "Unless you think they're going to let you get close enough to throw a punch." Ted watched Jack for a long moment, waiting for him to argue. When he didn't, he looked around the room at the parts before reaching for one at the edge of the table. "Now, unless you have an idea of where we're going to go now that our ride is conscious, bring me whatever electronics you have that I can take apart."

Harrison dragged his hands over his face and didn't remove them. A low groan echoed in the back of his throat as he rested his elbows against his knees. Where to go next was not a thing he wanted to think about right now. They didn't have a plan, they barely had anything to go on. And they didn't stand a chance against anything that they might be going up against at this point. He didn't know what he was supposed to do right now, dazed and confused and fighting back a migraine.

Even knowing what they'd done, he still would much rather have H&B go after Willow. After what he'd seen — knowing that it was *real* — he knew that they couldn't do anything to save them. Popping in and out was not going to work, not with Max like that. He could barely move on his own. Not even at the end.

Jack paced around the room and stopped suddenly. He picked up something and threw it down on the ground, sending pieces of it flying around the room. "There, you can have that," he said. "As soon as I can figure out where Mary is, we're getting out of here. I don't care what Willow wants with her, we're getting them back. At least, I am. I don't care if you follow me or not."

"She's going to open that damn portal again," Harrison said. His voice was quiet, though he did feel a gentle prod on his shoulder a moment later.

He looked up to see Jaime frowning at him. "The hell did you just say?"

Harrison scrubbed his face with his hands, letting his palms dig into his eyes. He really didn't want to think about what he'd seen, but he knew it was their best chance at figuring out what to do. Even if what most of them were thinking was a terrible idea, he didn't know what to do with what he'd seen. "Willow's taking them to the portal again. Thinks throwing Mary in is going to open it up for her. And then we can all hope she jumps in after her and we're done with it."

"You saw them again?" Jack was at attention now, the anger flaring for a moment so much that the ground shook. He seemed to realize what he was doing a moment later and everything was still once more. "How's Mary?"

Harrison shook his head. "It wasn't clear," he said. He didn't want to tell him about the bruises, or how weak she sounded as she talked. He definitely didn't want to tell Jack about her getting thrown into the ceiling so hard that it cracked.

Jack didn't say anything for a moment, though Harrison was fully expecting what did come when he spoke again. "So you know where they are. We can go get them."

"And have Willow kick all of our asses," Ally snapped back at him. "Or did you forget what she did to Adam. And you."

"*Mary* did most of that to me."

"Point stands."

"You're a bitch, you know that?"

"I don't know where they are," Harrison chimed in. He dragged the hands off of his face, looking back up and around at them. He felt tired, so very tired, but the throbbing in his head was being quickly replaced now with annoyance over dealing with all of them. "Max thought he knew the house, but it's not the same one. They're following the same route back, though. Somewhere about Washington. Getting close to Seattle."

"Where's the thing?" Jack asked.

"Canada," Jaime said, frowning. "We should get H&B to get them."

"We just broke out of H&B with two people they had intentionally put into comas," Ally pointed out. "You being one of them. I don't think they're going to listen to us right now."

"We aren't going to be able to rescue them on our own," Jaime said. "We could always just leave a message with what we know. They're a lot more concerned with tracking down Willow than any of us, so it should be—"

"Or they're going to come for us and throw us *all* in the coma room!" Jack snapped back at her. "Except Harrison. They'll make him stare at that fucking map again."

"And that's why you need to give me some time," Ted insisted. "I just need to figure out how this thing works and I will have something that might actually be able to help us."

"If it doesn't knock the rest of us out too."

"I don't see you coming up with any other ideas."

"We go in there right now, grab them, and then get out." Jack crossed his arms, leaning back against the wall and glared Ted down. "We don't need that many people to do it. Harrison and someone to watch his back."

"Someone like you?"

"Someone like *Jaime*," Jack continued. "The two of them, they could get shit done before, remember? We needed anything, they grabbed it and got out without anyone catching them. Only reason Harrison got caught last time was because Jaime wasn't there to make sure Willow couldn't see him. We pull the same trick again this time. You're overthinking this. We don't need to actually fight Willow, we just need to get them out of there. And once they're out, then H&B can do whatever the hell they want with Willow."

Harrison picked up the mug, his head swimming with everything as he tried to put together this plan and figure out if it was stupid. Firstly, he didn't know where they were. He'd said that. More than that, though, he didn't know what to make of the other parts of what he'd seen. Max and Mary were both doing so poorly that he wasn't sure they could really move them. Max couldn't even crawl without being in pain. Worse than that, Max was...

He didn't know if Max was even going to be himself the next time he saw him.

"Maybe we get lucky," Jack said. "Maybe she's not there. It's better than sitting around here and it's *certainly* better than calling in the people who tried to lock us up to keep us out of the way."

"Because they knew we were going to do exactly this."

"I don't think you saw all the people they had in the room," Jack reminded him. "It wasn't just these two. They threw Emma in there too. And Gavin. And Adam."

"Adam is missing an arm," Ted said. "They probably legit just moved him in so that he wasn't out in a hospital for any longer. But Emma and Gavin is weird."

Jaime prodded Harrison again, quiet now that the attention was off of the pair of them. "You don't look like you can do anything right now," she told him, keeping her voice low and tea in her hands. "Tell me this is a bad plan."

Harrison shook his head. "I don't know where they are," he said. "They might have moved by now."

And Max might not be Max right now. He didn't know what he would do if that were the case. Hell, he didn't even know how to put that into words. He wasn't even sure what he'd seen at the end, if that was what was really happening. Part of him hoped that he was wrong, that maybe that part was really just a dream, but it didn't feel like it. He kept his eyes down and on the tea in his hands instead, letting things happen around him instead. Jaime, thankfully, appeared to be willing to give into her own headache rather than pressing.

The conversation shifted without him to whether Ted's attempts to rebuild the machine was even worthwhile. Harrison put his mug down. He let himself curl up in the corner of the couch and drifted off to sleep. He wasn't sure if he could figure out where Max was if he tried, but he would have to wait to find out. The headache lulled him into a second slumber and he was more than willing to sleep off the rest of it.

CHAPTER EIGHTEEN

HARRISON AWOKE AGAIN still on the couch. The throbbing in his head had finally subsided, leaving him with an uncomfortable ability to think again. He knew already that he didn't want it, that the thoughts would only bring about realizations of things he didn't want to be true and uncomfortable decisions about what to tell everyone about what he'd seen. The want to think back on it was already battling with the fear of what he could find in those images and he tried to push it all aside, out of the way where he wouldn't have to dwell on it at all. He could just focus on the here and now.

It wasn't like he could do anything about it anyway. He didn't know where Max was beyond the vaguely familiar room. If he thought, maybe he could place it, but...

Next to him, Ally and Ted pored over the parts. They spoke quietly, passing things back and forth between them. A laptop was open next to them, Ally furiously typing between passing or attaching things. In front of him, the television was gone, the screen discarded to the side of the room while what he assumed the pieces of it were now scattered across the floor.

Portable knockout machine. They were making that stupid thing portable. Already, Harrison could see a problem with this idea.

"Tell me you aren't testing that in here," he said.

"We're turning it on again the next time Jack opens his damn mouth," Ted said.

"He's just frustrated."

"*I'm* frustrated," Ted snapped back at him. "I don't see *you* jumping up and offering people to go on a suicide mission unarmed."

"I haven't even been awake for most of this," Harrison reminded him. "Or was I talking while I was passed out on the couch?"

"You are so pissy when you wake up," Ted told him. "If you dreamed up another lead, though, keep it to yourself. Jack's still on this send Harrison and Jaime in and hope they don't die thing." He snapped something in place in front of him, his expression souring at the crack and his hands pulling away from the device.

Across from him, Ally shook her head and took it back from him, armed with tape, a bit of metal, and her fingers. He could smell the smoke and burning metal that followed, not quite sure what the thing they had assembled on the table was. Whatever it was, it looked like a mess, covered in loose wires and connections and something that was definitely still connected to the computer. The thing that knocked him out. They were trying to make it portable, and that looked... Well, they could pick it up at least. "Is that done?" he asked.

"Just about," Ted said. "Turns out most of the rest of it was just an amplification and limiting the effect of it. This here, this is what it actually is."

"It should still work, though," Ally said. "Just had to separate the part that actually did something out from everything else and make it take a battery as a power source without shorting the damn thing out. But if we need it, I think we can probably make another one. If we really need to."

"Have I been sleeping for a week? How long have you been working on this thing?"

Ted shrugged. "Well, I kind of lifted a couple schematics for it when I was looking through and finding stuff on Willow," he admitted. "So it's not like we're working blind on this. But apparently it's really not that complicated. It's just a frequency that affects us more than anyone else, really, and fed through a specific noise filter. It's not really like what Max does, it just kind of feels like it. It seems pretty straightforward, but there's a few things in here that Ally keeps saying is really weird."

"Because it *is* weird," she insisted, finally finishing whatever she was doing and putting the remaining wires down again.

"This thing should be designed to take a way stronger current than the one that it was dealing with. Why bother running it at half power?"

"Because half power meant that it already knocked out a room full of people. They didn't need it running any higher than that."

"But what if that's what got Willow up?" Ally pressed. "This all had to start somewhere. And Willow was in that room before, right? So if she was in that room and they had this kicked up the whole way to make sure it kept her down, what if it did something to wake her up? And *that* is why we're dealing with this now."

"Does it really matter *why?*" Harrison snapped. "She went and kidnapped Max. And Mary. And we're just sitting around here and can't even do anything about it but play with whatever that thing is and hope it somehow gives us a chance."

"Better chance than we had before," Ted told him. "But we do have to test it, and we kind of removed anything this thing had to keep it from spreading the sound outside of a certain area."

"How did you get around that when you got me?" Harrison regretted asking as soon as it was out of his mouth, but it was already too late.

Ted wound his hand through the air with more flourish than Harrison knew was necessary, the leftover liquid from his mug of tea spilling into the air and drawing close to Ted's face before he realized whatever his initial demonstration was might be a bad idea. He faltered as it got close before he decided against it and let it linger in the air for him to gesture at instead. "Muffled it," Ted explained. "Although it needs a *lot* to muffle the sound of it. And then we just turned it off once we got in there."

"Ted did, anyway," Ally offered. She unplugged the device from the computer, staring at it as if she wanted to try it out. Her fingers moved toward the device and lingered there for a moment before she put her hands flat on the table. She looked at Ted with a glare. "He went in with a damn fishbowl of water over his head. Because apparently you can breathe underwater now?"

"Testing gets a little weird," Ted said dismissively. "You're the one who can apparently solder with your fingers."

"Comes in handy."

"Was that a pun?"

Ally laughed, shaking her head and looking back down at it. "It needs some kind of casing," she said. "We're going to break it if we're carrying it around like this."

"Why does this feel stupid?" Harrison asked, looking at it. It didn't look like much of anything, really, just wires and speakers and a bunch of batteries, none of which he was sure actually connected to anything. He wasn't anxious to see them try it out, though he knew eventually Ally was going to get tempted to actually do it. Distraction was necessary before it got the better of her.

"Where's Jack and Jaime?" he asked.

Ally's hands relaxed. "Groceries," she told him. "Kind of stupid, though. It's not like we're going to be able to actually stay here long, right?"

"Maybe H&B isn't going to come looking for us," Harrison offered. "Priority is Willow right now, right? So long as we stay out of the way like they want, we'll be okay."

"We also took their two leads to finding her," Ted pointed out. "You disappeared, but Jack was stuck in there with Doctor Gethen for a while like he was going to tell them more. If they find out that you found out something new, you're getting dragged back."

"Great, this time we're *actually* hiding out from an actual mysterious organization," Harrison said, rolling his eyes and sinking back into the couch. "Remember when it was just Emma? Men in black, just worrying about being taken away and..." Harrison paused. "You know, I never knew what they were going to do. If they were supposed to murder us or take us in for experiments or whatever the plan was."

"I don't think it really mattered," Ally said. "We didn't really think that much about anything except where we were going. And I just accepted that whole portal to paradise thing." She shuddered. "She's really heading back there?"

Harrison looked back at her sharply. Right, he had said that hadn't he? He let out a groan, shaking his head and considering just going back to sleep again, hoping that this would all turn out to be another dream if he just didn't think about it. But it wasn't a dream, and now they were taking apart H&B property in an attempt to protect themselves. And Max was still gone, and about to be gone forever. If he wasn't already.

"Yeah," he said finally. Everything about him was tired and he didn't want to think about this right now. He wanted it to be a horrible nightmare, not their only lead. "Yeah, that's where Max thinks they're going."

"At least we know how to head them off," Ted offered. "We just have to get to the middle of nowhere before they do."

"How are they?" Ally asked. "Are they at least..."

Harrison shook his head before Ally could figure out her words, his eyes going down to the device on the table but looking far past it. "No," he said. Jack wasn't here to get mad about it, to demand that they do something about it, so he could be honest. He already felt guilty about leaving them there. "Mary's still fighting, but Willow's not pulling her punches."

They stayed very quiet for a moment, Harrison letting his eyes drift up to the kitchen. He was getting hungry, he realized, and it would be an adequate distraction from the thoughts in his mind for the moment. He disappeared from the couch and reappeared in front of the fridge, looking through it to find anything that he could shove into his mouth.

"We'll get them back," Ted told him. "We'll have to get H&B to do it, but we'll get them back. Did you happen to catch where they were?"

"No," he told them. There should be more in here, but Harrison could make do with the remaining pickles for now. He ate the first one and let himself think back on what he'd seen. "Max knew where they were. But I don't think he was right. He thought it was that princess looking room, the one where he bit the doll in half, but it was... it wasn't there."

"How do you know?"

"It wasn't right," Harrison said. He looked around to the cupboards, trying to see if there was anything else hidden in here to consume. The less he focused on what he'd seen, the easier it was to talk about. "It was close to it, but it wasn't the same place."

"If you really thought about it, you think you could figure out where it was?" Ally asked. "You figured it out last time, right?"

Harrison shook his head, still not looking at them. The pickle jar was empty now and he put it down on the counter. "That was something else," he said. Tara had done something and helped him figure it out, but he didn't want to drag her into this. Not now that they were once more on the run. "I won't be able to do that again."

"Do you have to?" Ted asked. He was on his feet, moving closer to the kitchen and to Harrison. He reached out like he might stop him from raiding the pantry, but thought better of it. "The first place you found. Where was that?"

"It was a building downtown."

Ted nodded. "And how close was it to the place where we met Max the first time?"

Harrison stopped, his hands hovering above the shelves as nothing was coming forward as potential edible material, and thought back on it. The building where Max had suddenly appeared as part of their group was a fancy apartment downtown. And the place Willow had brought them this last time...

"It was the basement of the same building," Harrison said. "How did I not notice that?"

Ted nodded slowly, glancing back at Ally. "So if they're heading back to the... I hate calling it the portal, but if they're heading back *there* again, then maybe they're taking the same path there, right? So we don't need to know *exactly* where they are. H&B already know where we stopped, so they just have to follow the same path again. And then they don't need us anymore."

"Which means we're not on the run anymore." Ally, at least, sounded happy about that. "And they know Willow doesn't want anything to do with us, right? So we can all just go home and let them deal with this."

"And then when they get Max back, you guys can finally talk," Ted added.

Harrison let out a sigh and closed the pantry, the last moments of what he'd seen playing over in his mind again. He nodded. "Maybe," he said.

"*Yes*," Ted insisted. "You guys need to at least talk."

"If he's the one that comes back."

The words were out before Harrison could stop them and he was careful not to look at them. They were a mistake. They didn't need to know about that, didn't need to know that Max was fading away from his own body or that Willow was intent on bringing Luke back through him. They didn't need to know that this particular plan appeared to be working, and that it looked like it was already too late to stop it.

Sudden clattering from the bedroom silenced them. Jack and Jaime were out getting groceries and would have used the door. There was no one else in here except for them. They froze, staring at the closed door. A second later it opened, Maya looking at all of them like she couldn't believe what she'd found.

CHAPTER NINETEEN

THEY DIDN'T DARE move, staring at Maya as she looked between each of them. There was shock on her face, followed by disbelief. Her eyes panned back and forth between them for several long seconds, her hands coming up in front of her but unable to put together quite what to say. Levi appeared behind her, looking over her shoulder at what was going on. He shoved her forward and she made way for him to join her.

"I can't believe you're this stupid," Maya said.

"I can," Levi said. He disappeared from Maya's side and appeared next to Harrison, hand grabbing his shoulder and waiting until Harrison was looking at him before he winked.

It was more of a fuzz that settled over Harrison's mind. It wasn't like what Gethen was making Devlyn do to him, more like when Max was just starting to get nervous about something. Harrison winced against it, wondering what he was trying to do. Levi took his hand off of him, turning to the fridge as Harrison stared at him. Something was strange here. They should be...

He didn't know where he was. Harrison looked around, vaguely aware that he had been here before, and had been here for a while now. He was sure that this was where Mary and Jack lived, but he didn't know *where* it was. And he wasn't sure where anything else was either.

"No running," Maya said, looking at Harrison as her hands moved. Her attention drifted around the room, counting the people there and noticing something off. "Where are the other two?"

"You don't have to take us back," Ally told her quickly.

"Not yet. Seriously, where are they?"

Ally struggled, her hands jerking as she moved them along with her words. "They're... out."

"Are they coming back?"

"Yes."

"Good." Maya dropped down next to her on the couch, side-stepping all of the metal around her. "We can hang out here for a while, then. This whole thing is getting stupid. They got any food?"

Levi shook his head.

"We know where Willow's going," Ally offered. "We can tell you and then you don't need us anymore."

"Nope," Levi said. He pushed Harrison forward, catching him as he stumbled and looping an arm around his shoulders to drag him into the living room with the rest of them. One handed, Levi continued. "Even if we gave a shit about where Willow was, we still have to bring you back. And *we're* stuck doing it because your actual Keeper's stuck on Willow duty."

"Gavin?" Ted asked.

"Emma."

Confusion crossed Harrison's face and he glanced at Ted and Ally. They said nothing, but he could tell they were all caught on the same piece of that. Emma had been in the room with Harrison and most certainly not out looking for anyone. Unless she had managed to wake up now that the machine had been removed from the wall and decided to continue doing what H&B told her after they had done that to her, she was likely still being held there.

"Why?" Ally asked, her words and her fingers slow to ask.

"Because they have history," Levi said, looking at Ally like she was not that bright. He let Harrison go, Ted stepping in to keep him on his feet while Levi bent down to look at her. "Emma didn't tell you about how she and Willow were a thing back in the day, did she?"

Harrison was paying attention. He unhooked himself from Ted's grasp, leaning against the wall as he tried to keep his balance, but his attention was on Levi as he moved between them, making sure they would all be able to see what he was about to tell.

Maya smiled and shook her head. "They don't need to know about this."

"We have some time to kill," he said. "Unless you want to come back here again to grab the other two. No one's told them we're here, have they?"

"Do I look like Devlyn? I'm not that sloppy."

Levi laughed, the sound foreign to them and doing nothing to put them at ease. Still, Harrison didn't feel like he was dangerous, even if he was doing something to knock out his sense of direction. Levi looked around to make sure he had their attention and started to move his hands. They stopped in the air and he looked back at them again, curious. "Actually, what *do* you know about the break out?"

A look passed between Ted, Ally, and Harrison. "Which breakout?" Harrison asked carefully.

"When we broke out of Lightstone. That complex in the middle of nowhere in BC."

Harrison knew the complex, but had no idea there was a name attached to it. That hadn't been important, and Emma hadn't told them much about what had happened back then. They didn't think to ask, sure that the memories were probably too painful for them to relive.

"Anyway," Levi continued, taking a moment to gesture for Harrison and Ted to sit down. Maya rolled her eyes and got out of the way so they could have the couch. "So about twenty of us were left at the end there. There was Rue with her cult and the rest of us. Then there was Emma, Adam, and Devlyn. Those three kind of floated between them. Emma was trying to convince Willow that Rue was full of shit, but somehow she got roped into it along with Adam."

"Somehow," Maya said, eyes rolling. "You couldn't separate those two before Rue got involved and shoved Luke in there. She knew Willow had a thing for him. And the only reason Adam went dark side is because of Luke. Really, the best thing Rue did was get Luke on her side."

"What's Luke got to do with Adam?" Harrison asked.

"They're brothers."

"What?"

"It's not that important," Levi said, brushing it off. "See, the genius thing with Rue was her idea of getting free was to toss everyone into the garbage and hope the afterlife was better. Which was the stupidest brilliant idea, because they did everything to keep us inside the complex, so they were totally not expecting them to go into a place they wouldn't be able to escape from. It was complete chaos, and it was enough to get the rest of us out of there."

"Most of us," Maya corrected him. "They *did* kill Sarah. And Rue didn't make it."

"How did the rest of you get out?" Ally asked.

"There were three people in charge of that place that kept us there," Levi said. "We don't know how they did it, but they had some way to keep us from doing too much if they didn't want us to. Devlyn killed two of them. Once they were dead, something snapped back in all of us and we could suddenly figure out how to teleport a lot farther away than before. Like, outside of the place. And then we all found out that breaking out of a complex in the middle of the woods isn't really the best way to start a new life. Especially when none of us could remember our old lives."

"At least we aren't still in there," Maya said.

Silence hung in the air as they took in the story. It was told so casually that Harrison wondered if some of it had been made up. He was still stuck on the idea of Adam and Luke as brothers, wondering why no one had said anything about that before. It didn't matter, he knew, but he felt like he should have known. Not that that was the only confusing part of the story.

Ted got to his feet and walked toward the door. He made it halfway before he stopped, feet lifting off the ground and Maya frowning at him. "What do you think you're doing?" she asked. "You aren't leaving. As soon as the other two get here, you're going right back to H&B."

"Just getting some water," Ted said, a smile across his face. "Couldn't leave if I wanted to, right?"

Maya smiled back at that, clearly not trusting him as she let him back down onto the ground. Ted met Harrison's eye and turned away from her, his hand making a small gesture that he hoped Maya didn't catch. "Distract them!"

"So…" Harrison said, struggling to come up with something. "What happened to the third guy? Or was it just the two guys who could stop you from doing… stuff?"

"Who knows," Levi said, looking to Maya. "We never even knew how they did it. We just couldn't figure out where anything was beyond Lightstone, so we couldn't get out of it. Your brain did weird stuff when they were around. It's weird, but I can't even remember what they look like now."

Maya shook her head. "They don't deserve to be remembered," she said. "Bastards, every one of them. Hope he's dead."

He could see Ted's hands moving out of the corner of his eye and Ally shifted next to him. Whatever was happening, he knew it was a terrible idea, but he didn't take his eyes off of Maya or Levi. He wished he knew what he was distracting them *from* but he trusted Ted and Ally to at least not make things any worse. At least, he trusted Ted not to.

"And now you're going to be throwing us into Hayes so H&B can keep us locked away," Harrison said.

Maya looked at him, curious and trying to piece together what he had just said. It was clear that she didn't see the parallel, though she was trying to figure out just what he was talking about. The parts were almost connecting, and she looked to Levi like he might be able to figure it out.

Harrison had never gotten that much out of an expression before. He tried not to think too much about it. "Why does H&B even want us?" he asked to distract himself. "Just because we left?"

Ted came back to the couch, glass of water in hand and something strange about him. Harrison only caught him out of the corner of his eye, but he wondered what this plan of his was.

"Oh, they think they can turn you guys like us," Levi said. "Into Keepers. That kid, Max? Apparently he was basically there, but if Willow's got him then they don't think they're getting him back. Mary was next, but she's gone too. Which means the next best bet is you guys."

"Apparently your friend, the one who works with Gavin, they had some luck with her," Maya said. "Not everything, not yet. But they put her in with Willow a couple times and she developed a couple extra things. Apparently just being in a room with her is enough torture."

Harrison jumped, a gasp filling his lungs as something cold crept into his ears. He forced it into a laugh, but neither of them seemed to notice. He shot a look back at Ted as his ears filled with water, wanting to dig it out as the sound around him muffled. He didn't even know water could get that deep in there, and it sent an uncomfortable chill up the back of his neck.

He could see now that Ted's ears shone with liquid inside of them, as did Ally's. While Ted was looking at him like he should be distracting them and sticking to the damn plan, he caught a look at what Ally had been doing. On the table, the device had been quietly plugged into the computer and she was not so idly working a few of the wires between her fingers until they were properly melted together.

This was a stupid idea.

"What is that thing?" Maya asked, coming over to look at the mess of a device on the table. "I didn't think those two were studying anything technical."

"Oh, this?" Ted asked innocently. Harrison could barely hear him through the water digging deep into his ears. "It's..."

Ally slammed something on the table.

A sharp sting of something cut through the water earplugs. Harrison winced, but it only lasted an instant. In front of them, Maya and Levi hit the ground with a thud he couldn't hear, but he could feel. For a long moment they watched, the silence sounding almost dense thanks to the flood in their ears, but neither of them moved.

Ally slammed her hand back down on the device and it was over.

All at once, the static echoing in his mind lifted and he realized what was happening. They were caught and they had to get away. *Now.* H&B knew where they were and they were more than happy to lock them up. They had to tell Jaime and Jack not to come back here, that they weren't safe and they needed to run.

The water snapped out of his ears and Ted was looking at him while Ally gathered up the machinery in front of them. "We need to go," Ted said.

Harrison nodded. He could tell where he was again, and he knew how to get out of there. He picked up his phone and texted Jaime before he grabbed both of them by their arms. "I know a place," he told them. "We'll meet them there."

CHAPTER TWENTY

ALLY AND TED said nothing when he missed the place by a block and they had to try again. He would have to figure out what was happening, but it would have to wait until after they weren't in the midst of a crisis.

His mind was spinning and he didn't know what to do. H&B were very obviously not on their side anymore and would not work with them, but they were still their best shot. They could take down Willow. If they could just wait for that to happen, then Harrison could go get Max and Mary once the coast was clear. Until then, they would have to lie low and hope H&B didn't whisk them away to be locked up in a cell somewhere.

Jack was not a welcome addition to his thoughts. They caught him and Jaime up as soon as they made it to the basement of the convenience store, a largely forgotten refuge for teenagers looking to run away for a night and have a little privacy. If it came to it, Jack knew how to open the back door into the place for an escape, even if it meant being caught on the security cameras.

"And how is this any *less* stupid than actually *doing something!*" Jack roared. "We know where she's going! We might as well get them out ourselves. Hell, if you guys won't, I'll go do it myself."

"You have no idea where they're going," Ally pointed out. "You left before we got this far."

Jack glared at her. "And whose fault is that?"

"Yours," Jaime said. "You shouldn't have come back."

Ally flushed a bright red, but Jaime was calm next to her and shaking her head at her phone. "We need to stick together and figure something out. Even if we can get them back, that doesn't help us figure out what to do about H&B."

"If we get them back, it all goes back to normal," Jaime said "They'll get Willow back on their own and they want someone as far along as Max."

"And then they decide to lock him up instead," Harrison said. "When did they even decide locking people up was a good idea? We were supposed to be free to continue our lives so long as they got to do their tests and we didn't say anything."

"It was Gethen," Jack said. "You *know* it was Gethen."

Jaime stiffened at the name before confusion settled across her expression and she forgot about whatever it was that was bothering her. She tugged at the collar on her shirt and shook her head, looking back and forth between the two of them.

"They won't lock him up," she insisted. "They aren't going to lock any of us up. They can't."

"You think they won't try?" Ted asked.

"I think they physically can't," Jaime said. "Now that Ted can pick a lock, there's nothing they can do to keep any of us there."

"Are you forgetting how they locked you and Harrison up in a room for days?" Ally snapped. She gestured at the mess of wires. "You think they only have one of these? This thing is written in *Python!* They could make another in their sleep if they wanted to. *Ted* could make one!"

"Hey!" Ted looked offended, though it was hard to tell how deep that had actually cut coming from Ally. "I figured out the specs before you did!"

Jack tugged Harrison's arm softly and leaned in close. He looked back at the rest as they devolved into an argument and then returned his eyes to Harrison. "We need to talk," he said. "I've been... I've seen Mary again."

Harrison nodded and they vanished.

———◆———

THIS TIME, HARRISON ended up exactly where he intended to. The street was nice and calm, and just a little too familiar. He brought them further out, far enough that H&B shouldn't even think of looking for them here. He remembered this place, the swing sets where Max had broken his leg so badly. They weren't far from where Max and Mary had been held when he saw them last. He wished he could have thought of a happier place to take them, but this was as pleasant as his mind could think of knowing what was coming.

Harrison didn't say anything, waiting for Jack to spit it out himself. He was already so tired from worry that he wasn't sure he wanted to know what he was seeing. What his dreams were showing him.

"Nice place," Jack said.

"Max got that compound fracture on those swings over there."

Jack nodded. The silence stretched on for a few more seconds before he spoke again.

"They're locking up Max as soon as they get him back."

Harrison nodded. "I know."

"Do you know why?"

"Just spit it out, Jack," he said. He was so tired.

"He's not Max anymore," Jack said. "Not really."

"I know." He kept walking, trying to not look at the swings. He turned them away from the house they were being held at, knowing that they were probably not there anymore. It had been too long now, and surely Willow would have moved them. He didn't want to think about this conversation, but he had agreed to it and he was stuck here now. "He's Luke."

Harrison let his eyes drift up, avoiding looking at Jack as he walked. The day was cool, the clouds hanging low in the sky overhead. Jack said nothing as he fell in step beside him. He let himself get distracted by the trees overhead and the cherry blossoms falling to the ground. With just how quiet it was in a neighbourhood that surely had a lot of children. With how they had veered back onto the path that he had walked with Max before.

With how he may never be able to talk to Max again.

His thoughts were going places he didn't like. He needed to get Jack talking so he didn't keep thinking. "How's Mary?" Harrison asked. He realized his mistake as soon as he said it.

"Not good," Jack said. "Still fighting, but I don't think she's got much left. Trying to keep Max around, though. She doesn't think he's beyond hope. She's trying to keep him there."

"And what if he's gone? Just gone, and all that's left is Luke?" Harrison didn't like hearing the words spoken, didn't like acknowledging that he was actually thinking about this. He didn't want to be thinking about this. He wanted to believe that Max was still there, that he was always there and that there was nothing wrong. That he would come back exactly the same as he'd been before. He stopped, trying to keep any more words from coming out. "What if…"

"Hey," Jack said. He put his hand on his shoulder and turned Harrison to face him. "Hey! You don't get to fall apart over this shit, Harrison. I am *not* going to be the only one who has to deal with all this shit, you got that? And you are going to get them back. You already found them once, all you have to do is keep it together long enough to grab them next time—"

"But what if that was it?" Harrison pressed. "What if that was the last chance to get him? And now he's just gone and Luke is—"

Jack's hand fell hard across the side of Harrison's face, the sound of the smack echoing in his ears. Jack flushed red, furious but still clearly trying to hold back. His hands went back to Harrison's shoulders, shaking him. "How many times am I going to have to smack some sense into you?" Jack yelled at him. "We are getting them *both* back, and if he's Luke, he's not staying Luke for long."

"You don't know—"

"*Yes I fucking do.*" Jack stared at him, jaw clenching as he clutched Harrison's arms tighter. He took a breath in and let it hiss out from between his lips, head tilting to one side like he was trying to crack his neck. "You didn't see what I saw," he said. "Mary's got it figured out. If Willow doesn't get to him, he doesn't go all Luke or whatever. And Luke doesn't stick around for that long when he is there. He can stick around ten minutes tops before he goes away again. Then it's all Max again. Look, all we have to do is head them off and grab them out of there and we're good. Both of them. While we still can."

"How did you..." Harrison let the question drop. The dreams, of course he knew because of the dreams. And he had to believe that Jack's dreams were just as real as his own. "How much have you been doing this if you know this much?"

"Like, every time I sleep," he said, his voice suddenly hushed. "I think Mary knows I'm there. She keeps talking to herself. I'm pretty sure she never used to do that. But at least she's still there. And Max is—"

"At least, she's still there."

"We're getting them back!" he snapped at him. "I will *punch that bitch in the face* if I have to and we are getting them back, do you hear me?"

Harrison laughed, his voice hollow and desperate. "And then what?" he asked. "Run forever? H&B is going to find us no matter where we go and Mary needs a hospital."

"*They both* need a hospital," Jack told him. "We'll get Max too."

"And then H&B will get them and we'll never see them again," Harrison said. Never mind that Max could hear Luke even when Willow wasn't there, that he seemed to be a constant presence in his mind. Never mind that Willow wasn't about to let him go without a fight. Never mind that he was sure the observations of someone in Mary's broken condition were probably skewed. Even if this worked and he was right, this was a doomed plan. "Or do you think they're going to just let them go?"

"They can't hold them. No contract is enough to let them keep us locked up against our will. And you know they can't actually keep us anywhere for long. Not if they want to run their little tests on us. Can't keep us locked away in a coma room for that. They can't do *shit* to us."

"They aren't going to lock you away."

Jack jumped away from him at the voice, turning wildly on Jaime like he was about to fight her. His eyes flew wildly around, looking for anywhere she might have come from, to Harrison like he might have seen her show up. He looked like he expected all of H&B to be right behind her, ready to swarm in on them.

Jaime had her hands up, looking calmly back at him and waiting for him to back down. Her eyes drifted over to Harrison, silently asking if he could believe he wasn't used to this by now.

Harrison was more than used to Jaime at this point that her appearance wasn't what was confusing. "You can teleport," he said. "When the hell did you learn to do that?"

Jaime shrugged. "Couple months ago. Are you going to punch me or are you good?" she asked Jack.

Embarrassed, Jack relaxed and let out a grunt, turning away. He started walking and they followed him. "You gotta stop sneaking up on people like that, Jaime. One of these days, someone's going to hurt you."

"I already got shot," she said. "You got worse than that?"

"You and Ally just don't know how to let something drop," he muttered. "What do you want? We were talking."

"You disappeared."

"I needed to talk to Harrison."

"You didn't need to leave to do that."

Already, Harrison could tell that this was going to go downhill. He needed to put a stop to this before it turned into something he would have to deal with. "You know Gethen," he said, grasping at the first thing he could think of.

Jaime stiffened and relaxed, her eyes searching the pavement. They said nothing as she came to a halt, letting her ponder as her mind worked in the circles it needed to. Her hands came up in front of her, fingers twitching in the air with the memory of a conversation never spoken. Finally, she let out a breath and nodded.

"Gavin mentioned him," she said. "Just once. He wanted me to sit in on this meeting and Gavin recognized him for just a moment. It was just for a minute and he looked like he was going to fight him. I could smell smoke. He might have tried to do something. But then he just kind of walked away. It was weird."

"What did he want with you?"

Jaime shrugged. "He wanted me to sit in on a meeting. I don't really remember much of it." She didn't meet either of their eyes as she said it, starting to walk again.

Harrison kept up with her, willing to let the matter drop, but Jack was less inclined. "How do you *not* remember dealing with that asshole?" he demanded. "What meeting needed *you* there for it?"

"It was about funding," Jaime said. It was clear to Harrison that something was coming back to her. Something that she didn't much like, and something that she didn't want to talk about. She could remember at least part of that meeting, and it was not a pleasant memory.

"You *definitely* didn't need to be there for a funding meeting."

"I didn't," Jaime agreed. "I... I left."

Something was strange about this. "Did you walk out?" Harrison asked.

Jaime stayed quiet for several steps. He could tell she was carefully considering whether to mention what she had just remembered. "No." She glanced back at Harrison, eyes narrowing for just a moment before she returned them forward. "You're starting to buzz."

"I'm what?"

"Try not to do that."

"I *can't* do that," Harrison insisted. "It might be something else around here."

"It's you," she said, looking around. "And Jack does it when he's sleeping. Trust me, it's my job to know these days. We need to go."

"Why?"

Jaime nodded down the street. "Devlyn," she said as if Harrison couldn't recognize the dyed hair or tattoos running up her arm from even this far away. She strolled as casually as she could despite sticking out in this neighbourhood, but her eyes were busy scanning every inch of the street around her. "I'm hiding us, but she'll hear you buzzing even if you're that quiet. Can you get us back?"

Harrison wanted to argue, but he didn't know how. He nodded and they left back to the basement.

———◆———

AS SOON AS they appeared, Jaime slammed her hands over both of their mouths to keep them quiet. At first, they weren't sure why. The room was darker than they had left it, and there were two people clearly moving in the shadows. It wasn't until they turned the light on that they saw who was there.

Levi and Maya had found them. Or rather, they had found this place. Ted and Ally were nowhere to be seen. Already, Levi and Maya's hands were moving, trying to work out why there was no one here and if they had the wrong place somehow. It looked like they had been told specifically to come here, though Harrison wasn't paying attention to them.

He nudged Jaime and pointed to the door. At the top of the stairs, the door leading into the closed store was left just a crack open, like someone had managed to get it open. Jack had seen it too and was nodding, looking like he might make a run for it himself. Harrison didn't wait for a reply before he teleported them up into the store above them.

Ally clutched the device in her arms, tools shoved into her pockets as she waited next to the door. Ted was next to her, his hand over the lock and looking frustrated that it wasn't doing what he wanted. He drew his hand back and the water followed it. It pooled in a ball in his palm and started to freeze before Ally let out a gasp, her eyes wide and ready to set something on fire to save herself.

She relaxed as soon as she recognized them. "We have to go," Ally signed frantically around the device.

"Where?" Ted asked. "They're going to find us again!"

Harrison didn't like what he was about to do, but it was the best he could think of. "Congratulations, Jack, we're going with your plan," he said, taking them all far away from here.

CHAPTER TWENTY ONE

EVERYWHERE THEY WENT, Levi and Maya found them. Every small house, every random street, every unfinished basement or dusty attic, they were there and they were not happy about the chase. They soon found that aiming for houses meant that the pair would knock on the front door first and, so long as one of them was paying attention, they could escape.

Harrison took the time to text his sister and tell her that he wasn't expecting any of this to go well. He didn't know what he was expecting. Either he was going to end up in a holding cell for H&B and doomed to never leave while they tried to see how much power they could milk out of him, or he would be far away from here with Max, never to return.

Or worse, he'd have to go back to his life like nothing happened.

The plan had changed several times already, but none of it affected what Harrison was doing. He just had to keep getting them away from Levi and Maya whenever they showed up, and their stops were usually coordinated with somewhere that they could rest. Ally and Ted could continue working on that device while Jack could try to get some sleep and see if he could find Mary again.

None of Harrison's dreams had Max in them, not that he slept much. Jack was very careful not to mention him when he talked about what he saw. It was clear to Harrison that he was only partially doing it to keep the secret of what Max was becoming. Jack just didn't want to tell him how much worse Max was getting, and that said volumes.

For the moment, they had stopped in the same house as before, the one where Emma had broken in and taken him away. The house with the pool where he'd regretted letting Max out of his sight. Every single one of these places was bringing back uncomfortable memories, but that wasn't why he felt so strange in here. They were in the basement, the house above them empty for the day but littered with signs that people were living here again.

Jack tried to convince them that they were leading Levi and Maya in to take care of Willow. That he was fine with not standing a chance against Willow, but they were clearly doing a terrible job of tracking her down on their own. That they were actually helping.

"Then don't you want to lead H&B *away* from them?" Ally demanded. "I thought they were planning to lock us all up!"

"We *need* to be there so we can get Mary away from them! I'm not letting her get locked up either."

Harrison couldn't quite pay attention to this house, but he did notice how Jack had stopped mentioning Max since he woke up this morning. He tried not to think too much about it and instead focused on how he said they hadn't moved. The last time, Max had confirmed that it was the same house with the pool, but Harrison was very certain they were not upstairs. Maybe if he could concentrate, he could figure out where they were.

"You're going to get *all* of us caught at this rate!"

"If they show up, you can just do whatever you did last time to knock them out. And if that doesn't work, you can set them on fire. You're good at doing that to people."

"Oh, would you get over that?"

It was something about this place, Harrison decided, that was making it so hard to focus. It wasn't the people around him yelling loudly enough to make the neighbours aware of their presence, or the knowledge that Levi and Maya were likely only a short way from finding them once more. There was something else about this place, something familiar. And getting loud.

"You see my face?" Jack demanded, pointing at the scars as he inched toward her. "I don't *have* to get over it!"

"Can you both calm the fuck down?" Ted asked, looking over the device. "If anyone comes home, we're going to have to deal with *cops*."

He looked around at each of them, staring a moment at Jaime before he looked up into the corner of the room. Jaime wasn't paying attention, but Harrison was sure she would be able to hear it if she tried. And that she would agree that it definitely sounded familiar. More than that, he could almost tell where it was coming from.

"One moment," he said.

Harrison appeared on the street and realized a moment later that he shouldn't have done that. He might be caught by some random onlooker. Not that it mattered. He wasn't going back to H&B willingly after this. Even if Levi or Maya or Devlyn had managed to find him standing here, appearing out of thin air, he wasn't going to get caught. Not now. Not when he was this close.

In front of him, he knew he'd found it. Every house on this street was the same, as far as he was concerned. They looked the same besides the colour, each of them sitting so far apart from their neighbours that you might forget that you'd already seen this house before. But they each had the same bay window at the front, each had the same front door painted a different colour, each had the same backyard. But this one only two doors down from where they were now, this one with different curtains in every window to match the different coloured rooms inside the house as if it were trying to be different from the rest, he knew it was the right one.

A little closer. Just a little closer.

He went to the back of the place. There was an above ground pool here too, just like every other house on this street, one that he was careful to slip behind. He couldn't see any movement inside and didn't know where they might be. But he could still hear them. He knew they were there.

It was mostly Mary that he was hearing from inside there, but whispering through that static that Mary was letting out, Harrison could still hear Max. He was still there. He had a chance.

Harrison was back in the house a moment later, appearing directly behind where Jack had been standing. He was glad he wasn't missing anymore, because that was going to be important. He grabbed Jack's shoulder and pulled him back. Jack jumped, but Harrison didn't let go. "Found them. You still in?"

"Right now," Jack said.

"No!" Ally snapped at them, turning on Harrison and grabbing him. "*You* can't leave. If H&B find us—"

"You turn the machine on," Harrison told her, pulling himself away. "Or tell them to come join us. We'll probably need the help."

She stared after them as they left, but Harrison wasn't bothered by the look of betrayal, and that underlying sense of concern. Either they were getting Max back, or they were not coming back at all, and Ally seemed to understand that more than Harrison did.

CHAPTER TWENTY TWO

HARRISON DECIDED THE bedroom he'd spotted from the street was likely a safe place to start. He hadn't seen any movement in it, in any event, and the large bay window had been drawn. Now that he was inside, it looked like a grand room that had been untouched by a madwoman and her two broken hostages that she had been dragging across the country.

Neither of them was paying much attention to what was going on, Jack snapping around to try and find any sign of life in the room. It was quiet in here except for the sound of static echoing in their heads. Harrison could already tell that Jack could hear Mary in there. It was hard not to. But their ears were picking up nothing of where in the house they might be held.

"Where are they?" Jack asked, his voice silent and his hands moving. "Mary's here somewhere."

Harrison nodded. "Have to find them," he signed, keeping just as quiet. "If Willow finds us, bring the house down."

Jack nodded a little too enthusiastically. For all his bravado, he was anxious about running into Willow. That mix of hatred and fear, of knowing exactly what she had done to Mary and both wanting to get back at her for it and not wanting to be subjected to it himself, was playing inside of him. If he ran into her, he was more likely to bring down the house out of survival instinct than out of any intentional malice.

Jack turned and jumped, someone standing in front of him. Jaime clamped her hand over his mouth before he could make a sound and held it there until his shoulders finally relaxed. "You're both idiots," she signed. "You're going to get killed."

Whatever he was going to say, Jack decided it wasn't important. He shook his head, jaw clenched as he walked past her and out of the room. He waved for them to follow, every move impatient and aching for this to be over. Harrison understood. They were so close now, and he just wanted to find Max and get him out of there. It had been too long, and he had heard his voice. He hoped they weren't too late already.

At any other time, they would have mentioned that this place was hideous on the inside. Every room had a different colour scheme, each drawing off of a different neutral palette with a different accent colour. Harrison only noticed to keep his mind off of the worry and from listening too closely to the static. He didn't want to know that they were about to be caught, and didn't want to know what else he might find out if he paid too close attention to the buzzing in his mind.

Even with Jaime, they moved slowly and carefully through the house, Jack looking around carefully at each of the rooms like he was trying to pick them out. "What are you looking for?" Harrison asked as they got to the bathroom. Jack threw the door closed and Harrison leapt forward to stop it from slamming. Everything was quiet so far, but that didn't mean Willow wasn't in here somewhere.

"Blue curtains," Jack said. "There were blue curtains."

Harrison thought about it, his mind going back to the outside of the house. Every room was different, which made it easy to pick out which one that might be. Harrison nodded and waved them close, trying to figure out where the room was in relation to where they were now.

It was a spare room, littered with hobbies and resolutions that were never kept. Crafts that were half forgotten, scarves only partially knit, and a treadmill that looked like it had been used for a month before being discarded. In here, the blue curtains were drawn to hide the shame of it all, but also to hide the young woman lying in a small heap under the desk pushed to the side of the room.

"Mary!" Jack forgot about any need to be quiet, going to her side and prodding her awake. Even sleeping, she looked like she was tired. The circles under her eyes were so dark they might have been bruises, which they well may have been. She was covered in small abrasions, her clothing marked with dark brown spots where the blood had dried, and most of her skin was a marble of different colours. Harrison wondered how much worse she might have been if Max hadn't been here. His mere presence was usually enough to help heal some of the harsher injuries she must have been hiding.

But Max wasn't here. Harrison looked around the room, but there was no sign of someone else in here. Small piles of cloth and yarn and paper weren't large enough to hide another person. Harrison moved away from them, looking to the adjoining washroom, but there wasn't anyone in there. There were towels there, dirty and covered in dirt and dotted with blood, but nothing large enough that he could even mistake it for Max.

"Mary, come on, don't fucking do this to me," Jack muttered from the next room. "Come on, *wake up.*"

Harrison came back, looking back to see Mary. He could hear her, even if she wasn't responding. She was alive, and that static coming off of her was strong enough that he was starting to feel dizzy just being around it. "I can't find Max," he said. "I'm going to—"

"No," Jaime said, grabbing him by the arm before he could start exploring the rest of the house. "Jack," you know what's going on. Where's Max?"

"He was in here too," Jack said, continuing to gently prod Mary awake. His head bobbed in the direction of the corner. "He was over there."

But he wasn't here now. Harrison's mind was spinning with possibilities, none of them good. "Was he moving?"

Jack shook Mary one more time before he started to pick her up. "Yeah," he said. Harrison could tell that was only partially true, but Jack would not say anything more than that.

"You can take them back, Jaime," Harrison said, turning back to the door. "I'll meet you there."

"I can't take other people," Jaime said. "You'll have to—"

Willow appeared between them. None of them moved, terrified that she might be able to tell where they were. She looked around the room, brow furrowed in confusion, looking at each one of them and passing them over as irritation flooded her face.

Draped over her shoulder like a fresh kill was Max.

She was looking for Mary, and she knew just how to find her. Even if she couldn't see her, she could still hear her loud and clear. Willow looked back to where Jack and Mary were, a smile crossing her face as she looked directly at them.

Harrison bit back his warning. It was already too late, he knew, and Jack rose into the air by his neck. Willow still couldn't see him, thinking it was Mary that she had caught. Jack let Mary drop back to the ground, a low groan escaping her as she struggled to open her eyes.

You can't hide from me.

The voice was in his head, but he knew the words were Willow's. He didn't know how he had heard it, nor did he care. Jack's eyes were wide as he stared her down, his jaw straining and muffled sounds barely making it out of him as he struggled in the air to move. The ground around them shook, throwing Harrison to the ground as Jack threatened to bring the house down around them.

Across the room, Mary's eyes flew open, her body resisting every movement as she looked up to see Jack hovering over her. "No," she said, her word barely louder than a breath but Harrison could hear it louder than the cracking of the walls around them.

It wasn't the first time he had heard Jack scream like that, he knew, but he had never wanted to hear it again. He knew the smell as well, far too familiar with that initial scent of scorched clothing before the fire caught onto flesh. The ground stopped shaking in that instant and Harrison could only stare in horror as Jack was engulfed in flames.

Jaime was on her feet and leapt forward as soon as she could get her footing, launching herself at Willow. One leg swung up, catching Willow directly in the stomach with more force than he thought Jaime could muster.

Willow winced and Jaime flew across the room. She crashed into the already crumbling wall and crumpled to the ground. When she didn't get up, Harrison knew they were caught.

Slowly, Willow looked around the room. She looked bewildered, wondering when she had missed so many people showing up in here and what they wanted. Not that it mattered to her, but she didn't like that they had all snuck up on her. It was like she thought they were going to take her back to H&B, to lock her up once more. And she was going to take her time showing them why they weren't going to take her back.

Jack dropped to the ground on top of Mary. The flames were out, but she still jumped and groaned, struggling to get out from under him. He was still warm, even if he wasn't moving, and it hurt to have him on top of her. She was near tears, not sure if he was alive and in pain herself, looking around in confusion like she wanted an answer.

Harrison couldn't give her one. They were caught, and in trouble. They had to get out of here. Now.

But she still had Max. He hadn't moved from her shoulder, even as she had fallen. She kept a tight grip on him, and he needed to get him away too. All of them. Jack had said they were getting Max out of there too. But now Jack was likely not going to wake up for a long while to keep any of those promises.

And Willow was looking directly at him.

They needed to get out of there now. Everyone else was too far gone, too in need of a hospital or too unconscious to get out of here on their own. And maybe, just maybe he could get Max out of there with the rest of them. He scanned the room, tagging where each and every one of them was. All of them, even Max, were going to come with him. Even with Willow holding onto him, maybe he could drag him away as well. He marked all of them and he disappeared back to safety.

If this didn't work, he would be back. He would come right back and he was getting Max back himself.

CHAPTER TWENTY THREE

THE DIFFICULT THING about teleporting with things he wasn't in physical contact with was the landing. It was a lot harder to make sure everything ended up where they were meant to, and he was dealing with a bunch of people who weren't able to stand on their own. Panic didn't help, and he landed on something that moved under him as he appeared. Harrison collapsed to the floor, his eyes darting around the room to see if everyone made it.

Jack and Mary were in a tangled heap on the ground on one side of the room. Jaime didn't move on her own, though someone else under her did. There were voices around him yelling, but he paid no attention, continuing to look around. He got the other three out.

Max wasn't there. He had to go back.

Harrison tried to push himself up from whatever he had fallen onto, but it didn't stay still. From behind him, a tattooed arm reached around his shoulders and held him in place. Devlyn's face appeared beside his own and smiled, her expression tight and frustrated. She would much rather he not fight this, and she was going to do what she had to in order to make him comply.

He could get out like this. He could slip away while she wasn't holding him too tightly, while she hoped that he would submit quietly. Or he could have if Devlyn wasn't taking precautions.

As Levi had done before, Devlyn managed to get into his head and disrupt his sense of where he was. He winced against it, like it would do anything to kick the feeling out of his mind and give him back his ability to leave, but Devlyn didn't let him go. She dragged him to his feet, giving him a moment to look around.

They were caught, that much was clear. Jaime had dropped on Ted, who was now trying to figure out just what had happened to her. Ally was hovering over her, scared to touch her and looking back at Harrison like he might be able to give her an answer. Maya was there with them, keeping them from going too far and letting them look over Jaime.

On the other side of the room, Levi started to drag Jack off of Mary. He pulled a hand back when he touched him, confusion crossing his face before he decided he didn't need to use his hands at all to untangle them. Mary's head lolled to one side, groaning as she tried to maintain consciousness. She looked like she was having trouble keeping her eyes open, but her lips were moving, muttering something in a steady stream that Harrison couldn't hear. Not that he had time to listen.

"I need to go back," Harrison told Devlyn. He pulled away and Devlyn let him go, looking him over with a frown. "I saw him. I can get him back. You have to let me go back."

"You're not going anywhere," she signed, though she looked apologetic. "Sorry, but you're in some shit, Harrison. H&B want all of you detained for breaking your contracts. You gotta learn to be more subtle."

"Willow is just over…" Harrison tried to point, but he couldn't figure out which way was which. He couldn't place where the house was or where he was. He could barely place where his feet were under him and staying on them was a challenge. "She's close!" he snapped. "She's got Max and… and we can get him! Please, just let me go back for him."

Devlyn shook her head and tried to reach out for him. Harrison stepped back, trying to smack her hand aside. He tripped over his own feet and fell backwards onto the ground.

"We're not going on some witch hunt for Willow," Devlyn told him. "We're only here for you. But…" Devlyn said, looking back around the room. "If you want to tell us how you managed to get Mary back and what the hell happened to everyone, I'd love to hear it."

"*Willow happened*," Harrison yelled at her. "You need to let me go back for him!"

"No."

Harrison stared back at her as she towered over him. She didn't like it much either, but she didn't know Max. She didn't really know Harrison. It made it a lot easier for her to try and stick to her job, but she wasn't fond of letting Willow go if she was close. She couldn't let Harrison go, but once they turned all of them over, she would consider going out to look for Willow herself. But for right now, she had an unfortunate job to do.

Harrison wondered if he was buzzing, because he was pretty sure he shouldn't be able to tell that much about what Devlyn was thinking by just looking at her face. So long as she wasn't catching it, he might be able to do something. If she felt bad, if she was willing to go look, maybe he could convince her to get Max for him. Or let him take her there. He had to do *something*.

Max hadn't been moving. He hoped it wasn't too late.

She offered her hand and he took it, letting her help him to his feet. She kept hold of his hand, watching him carefully as he tried to find his balance on his own two feet. He made himself find that balance. There was too much happening, but at the very least he could keep his feet under him.

"What's going to happen to us?" he asked. He needed to keep her talking, to stall long enough for a plan to happen. Maybe if he could make her feel bad enough, she would take action, but he didn't know how to do that.

"How about you tell us what happened to them?" Ally snapped from the corner. "You can't just say Willow and leave it at that!"

"Not sure," Devlyn said. "Doctor Gethen wanted you guys specifically. He's on his way here to see you himself."

"You know people live in this house, right?" Ted asked from across the room. "They're going to come back and wonder why the hell there's a bunch of people in their basement."

Harrison's eyes stopped as they panned back across the room, finding the mess in the middle of it before they landed on Devlyn. Scattered across the floor was a plan that he could cross off before he even thought of it. The device that had knocked out Levi and Maya before was now in pieces on the ground, as far as he could tell. It already looked like a mess of wires and mechanics before, but they were strewn farther about now, probably not connected in any meaningful way any longer.

He was trying to make her feel sorry for them. Trying to get her to go and look in on Willow now. He needed to think of how he could do that. "Doesn't he want Max too?" Harrison pressed. "It wouldn't be that hard to get him. He's not that far away. I can show you where."

"No," Devlyn said, her expression softening. "I'm sorry. I really am. But really, we're just here for you guys. There's other people already tracking down Willow."

"But she's—"

Harrison cut himself off, feeling himself flush red as he tried to bite back the rest of his words. They were so close to catching her. There were three of them and Willow was so very close by, but they wouldn't even let him go and do anything about it. And Max hadn't been moving. He couldn't forget that, and couldn't help but fear that it was too late. That waiting here for this long meant that Willow had taken out her frustrations on him while he couldn't fight back. If he could fight back at all even when he was awake. If he could wake up at all.

It wasn't too late. It couldn't be too late. They were too close.

Devlyn sympathized, feeling more like she would at least try to see what she could find after they had been passed off. She would not go a moment before, knowing that if she left, Levi and Maya would likely be outwitted by them once again. They were already in enough trouble for letting the chase last this long and letting them escape at all. She would rather they not deal with another reprimand.

"If you guys are done," Levi said, pushing his way between the two of them to talk to Harrison. "Why is he hot? The burns tell me he didn't suddenly learn how to set things on fire."

"Willow," Harrison repeated. At least the dizziness Devlyn was causing him helped to keep him from sounding too angry about having to say it again. "We found her."

"Yeah, we got that," Ally snapped back at him. "What *happened?*" She thought that Harrison had brought Jaime with them and that it was his fault she was now unconscious and covered in drywall. If not for the Keepers here to take them away, she would have done more than yell at him. She didn't know what, but this felt inadequate.

"I didn't ask Jaime to come with us!" Harrison yelled back at her. He didn't have time for this. Someone needed to get back there now, and if he wasn't going to do it, then he needed to make sure Devlyn did. Before it was too late.

"We believe you," Levi said, clearly just wanting them both to shut up. "Just want to know what happened so we can figure out what to do next. Maybe go and visit Willow?"

It was a ploy, but Harrison would allow it. Maya was already shoving Ally down onto the ground to keep her from another outburst, indicating that he should be focusing on getting Mary to come around instead of picking fights. She was just happy they were all here and in one place, and she needed to keep them that way until Gethen showed up.

Harrison wondered if this was what reading minds was supposed to be like. Not words, but impressions of intent. Not that it mattered right now.

"We found Mary," Harrison told them, eventually settling his attention on Devlyn. She was the one closest to wanting to go there and actually do something. "And then Willow found us. And— and I guess she couldn't see us, so she set Jack on fire thinking he was Mary trying to hide from her. And Jaime tried to stop her, but she threw her into a wall. And she had Max. If you go now, you can get him back too."

Devlyn was about to do it. Her expression was sympathetic and her eyes flickered back to Levi and Maya, considering whether or not they could just keep Harrison here while he went to look at it. If nothing else, they could give the people looking for Willow a heads up of where she was if Harrison was right. Which, given who he'd brought back, he likely was. Even if she did run into Willow, she doubted she would cause nearly as many problems as she had been led to believe.

She pursed her lips and took a deep breath. She'd do it. Gethen was almost here and they could probably keep Harrison from going anywhere for at least a few minutes. She would only be gone a moment. "Levi," she said, nodding him closer. "Could you..."

Silence settled over them. Harrison looked around to find all three of the Keepers had gone very still in the last moment, staring ahead and not moving. They were not relaxed, looking more like they had dropped everything to stand at attention and were now waiting for instructions.

In that instant, the haze over his mind had even lifted and he could tell where he was. More importantly, he could tell where he wanted to go.

He looked between everyone else, seeing nothing but confusion reflected back at him, and the sound of a car in the driveway. None of them moved, not sure what to do. Even with everything that had happened and all the things they had seen, this was unsettling. Ally got to her feet slowly, leaning over like she was about to poke Maya just to see if she would react.

Mary was slowly coming around, letting out a small groan as she continued to mutter something. A warning. She didn't want them to go back, wanted them all to get away now. That they should let H&B deal with it and that he wouldn't like what he was going to find there. It was already too late and it wasn't worth it any longer. That it was too late for Max and she was so very sorry that she couldn't have done more.

But the Keepers weren't moving. They wouldn't stop him. No one would stop him.

He wouldn't question it. He had to go get Max. Now.

CHAPTER TWENTY FOUR

W<small>ILLOW WASN'T THERE</small> when he reappeared in the blue room. Seeing it now, it was amazing that nothing had happened to any of the houses only a few doors down. The drywall had cracked and the ceiling sagged above him. The windows had shattered at some point, leaving broken glass littering the ground, and everything inside had fallen over and been tossed around. He wasn't sure how much of the damage was from Jack and how much had come from Willow after they left, but it didn't matter. That wasn't what he was here for.

Amidst the wreckage, Willow left Max behind. He was propped up against a wall and not moving. His head fell to one side, his red hair matted with sweat against the side of his face, and his hands rested at his sides looking red and calloused after however long he had been trapped for.

Harrison went to his side, hands on his face and trying to see if he was okay. He didn't know how to check a pulse, to see if he was breathing, to do anything that might be useful right now.

Max was the one who knew how to do all of that, and he was in no condition to even tell Harrison what to look for. Harrison took his face between his hands, gently tilting it to look at him.

Max was cool under his fingers. Was that bad?

"Hey," he said, his voice barely a whisper. His heart pounded in his chest and he didn't want to breathe too hard. He had to be okay. He'd just gotten him back. It didn't matter that Max had broken up with him the last time they saw each other. He needed to at least know he was okay. "Come on, Max. You're okay. Tell me you're there."

Breathing. He was pretty sure Max was breathing. With his face so close, he thought he could feel something passing over his cheek, however faint. That was something, at least. He wasn't dead.

"You're okay, Max," he said, his voice a little stronger now, but still quiet. The moment of relief was quickly overshadowed by knowing just where they were. Alive meant little if he didn't remain that way. "Come on, we need to get out of here."

He knew Willow would likely be back at any moment. He didn't knew why she was gone now, but he didn't trust her to stay gone for much longer. Max looked so fragile, like he might break if Harrison tried to pick him up. Willow had not been careful, he remembered, and he knew moving him would be a risk he had to take. It was better than staying here. His breathing was so shallow and he was in desperate need of a hospital.

But H&B was looking for them now. He didn't want them to be locked up for the rest of their lives.

"Come on, Max," Harrison urged him. He was breathing and that was enough. They had to go now, before Willow came back. And they would go somewhere that H&B would not find them, somewhere that he could get medical attention. There had to be something. Somewhere.

His mind was spinning, but nowhere came to mind. He raced through the options, but every hospital and doctor he knew of would be too easily tracked down. Every crazy idea was to a place he didn't know how to get to. He thought of the cabin in the middle of the country, left abandoned most of the year. If he could get there and find a doctor, maybe that would be far enough. Maybe they wouldn't find them.

"Just tell me where," he said. He shook him gently, then remembered Max telling him not to shake someone until he was sure they didn't have any spinal injuries. He withdrew his hands quickly, changing his mind and shifting beside him. Technically he didn't have to hold him at all, but he wanted to be sure the landing didn't make things any worse. "You need to wake up, Max," he said, his arms reaching under Max's legs and around his shoulders to pick him up. "I don't know what I'm doing. It's your turn to figure this out. Where are we going?"

Harrison hadn't gotten to his feet when Devlyn appeared in front of him, looking up from the phone in her hand. That, Harrison knew, was Jaime's phone. She froze, watching him with lifeless eyes. Whatever sympathy she had for him before, it was gone now. He couldn't get a reading off of her, but he didn't need to. He already knew what she was here for.

He hadn't realized how quiet Max actually was until that moment. The static came flooding into his mind, and it was comforting to feel. More than knowing he was breathing, the static meant that Max was alive. It hit him hard, feeling like a promise that things were going to be okay.

It sounded strange, but he didn't want to think about that.

The look on Devlyn's face changed, Devlyn's red eyes blinking and the life flowing back into them. She took a step back and he could see from the look on her face that this was not she had been expecting. She thought she would find the house empty, that Willow might have already left with Max and that she could gently convince Harrison to let them handle it. Instead, her eyes panned over the destruction and the unconscious young man in Harrison's arms. She felt bad for not stepping in sooner.

"It's not safe here," she told him, looking pointedly at the beams that jutted out of the ceiling. "This house looks like it could come down on us."

Harrison shook his head, holding Max closer to him. "We're not getting locked up," he said.

"They won't actually do that," Devlyn tried to assure him. "I'm bringing you back one way or another. If you come on your own, we don't have to risk Max getting hurt anymore."

Devlyn knew it was wrong as soon as the words were out, but that didn't stop her from looking at him like this was his problem. Harrison held Max close, trying desperately to come up with somewhere else that they could go. *Anywhere* else.

His first thought didn't bring them far away. They were back up in the large bedroom on the top floor with the bay window, the ground creaking below them as Harrison added weight to a very precarious situation. He felt like one move might send them through the floorboards.

"Come on, Max," he said quietly, trying to gently rock him awake. "You're okay. We just need to get out of here. Where are we going?" Everything in his head was panic and static and the desire to get out of there as fast as they could without a location that was safe. He looked down at Max, hoping that he could wake up and just make this one choice for him.

Max wasn't moving, but Harrison could stil tell what he wanted. Somewhere in the static, Max was still in there and aware of what was going on, but he was very quiet and fading away more with every passing moment. He wanted Harrison to run, to leave before it was too late. He was screaming for Harrison to get out of there, that it was dangerous and he couldn't keep him back anymore. Not to be fooled because as soon as she got back, it was already too late.

That she was coming. That it was too late. That he was sorry. *I can't stop him. He's going to...*

Harrison tried to give him the slightest of shakes, to try and make him stay just a little longer. No matter how he tried, how he strained to hear, he couldn't hear him any longer in the static. Max was gone.

Devlyn was no longer in front of him. Out of nowhere, she went flying across the room and crashed head first into the window. He didn't see if she had fallen, his attention squarely on the person who had did it to her.

Willow.

He didn't have a chance. She was already in front of him. Willow didn't even look at Harrison, not caring that he was in the process of taking Max back. She placed two fingers on Max's head, looking like this was nothing more than an annoying chore.

The current ran through Harrison's body, making him see white. He thought he smelled his eyes burning from the inside. Every nerve ending caught fire and he tried to hold Max closer as he lost control of his limbs. Every muscle clamped down, from his fingers to his heart, refusing to obey him. They twitched on their own, his muscles crying out as the moments stretched into hours. He heard his own voice scream from somewhere very far away.

There was nothing else after that.

ABOUT THE AUTHOR

TANYA LISLE IS a novelist from Metro Vancouver, British Columbia, who has series littered across genres from supernatural horror to young adult fantasy. She began writing in elementary school, when she started turning homework assignments into short stories and continued this trend well into university. While attending Simon Fraser University, she developed an appreciation for public domain crossovers and cross-platform narratives. She has a shelf full of notebooks with more story ideas than pens lost to the depths of her bag. Now she writes incessantly in hopes of finishing all of them.

Thankfully, her cat, Remy, has figured out how to shut off Tanya's computer when she needs to take a break.

Printed in Great Britain
by Amazon

10665150R10141